The
Lost
Art

The Lost Art

Ryan Adkins

ARCHWAY
PUBLISHING

Archway Publishing books may be ordered through booksellers or by contacting:

Archway Publishing
1663 Liberty Drive
Bloomington, IN 47403
www.archwaypublishing.com
1 (888) 242-5904

Images by Ryan Adkins.

ISBN: 978-1-4808-1669-5 (sc)
ISBN: 978-1-4808-1670-1 (hc)
ISBN: 978-1-4808-1671-8 (e)

Library of Congress Control Number: 2015904527

Print information available on the last page.

Archway Publishing rev. date: 4/15/2015

Acknowledgments

Anthony Liggins: Thank you for all of your inspiration and support. You have truly had an influence and impact on both my career and the way I view, experience, and share art with others. I am a true supporter of your work, not just for its content but also for the volumes its messages speak. Your influence helped mold the character of Anthony Pastel within the story, as you have been both a mentor and a teacher to me. I hope to share my own stories and messages with the world—as you have and will continue to do—as we both move toward the future with a passion for moving others through art!

Jarryd Dollard: Cousin! Thank you for all of your feedback and bouncing of ideas when I first started out writing this story. You really helped me get the ball rolling and convinced me that this story was worthy of being told!

Family and Friends: Thank you for all of your love, prayers, and support. You have no idea how much inspiration I draw from you all, as so many of you have played such integral roles in my life. Family, thank you especially for living such hardworking and dedicated lives so that I have the opportunity to pursue my own dreams and goals in life. Friends, thank you all for listening to my crazy ideas and lifting me up when I need it the most!

Contents

Preface

Many years back—further than I can even remember—I had a dream: what if I had a magical paintbrush that allowed me to bring art to life? Of course I had no idea at the time that this crazy fantasy conceived by my overactive imagination would ever blossom into what would someday become a full-length novel. As I grew older and honed my understanding of the world, I began to develop a strong spiritual connection to art and began to realize something—what is this world but merely one big canvas just waiting for each and every individual to make his or her mark on it? I firmly believe that everyone has a piece to add in life's grand design; however, it is up to the individual to decide what he or she will spend his or her life painting.

Transversely, this novel is not only a reflection of my personal connection to art but also an opinion of where I believe art stands in the world today. *The Lost Art* is a commentary on the state of art and its diminished value in today's society. Art, which was traditionally considered a thing of high society, has become mainstream and, in many ways, watered down and depreciated among audiences. *The Lost Art* is a celebration of the evolution of art, paying homage to some of history's most acclaimed artists and works with a modern spin through the introduction of urban art forms and artists, bringing together the past and present.

Often viewed as simply vandalism, graffiti art serves as the perfect bridge between today's youth and art's rich and still relevant history. By introducing a main character that is a "tagger," a practice popular among graffiti artists, Huey's story effectively connects those who may be interested in art history but prefer more contemporary subject matter. The main character's story of self-discovery also speaks to what can be accomplished through the hidden talents of our youth that can be unlocked simply through believing in them and their abilities, a testament that many of our youths today can relate to.

My hope for this novel is that it touches the spirits of those who share my ideals concerning the irreplaceable role that art plays in our lives. No matter what background or walk of life you may be from, may this story inspire you to embrace your inner artist and leave your mark on this world, creating an everlasting story that will transcend both time and space.

Chapter 1
Painting the Town

Huey

In all our deeds, the proper value and respect
for time determines success or failure.
-MALCOLM X

The Arts District was once an urban wasteland—desolate and abandoned, a battered cocoon of a city filled with colorless people and uninspired dreams. No place for someone with a bright future, to say the least. Outsiders rarely visited, and for good reason. While some areas of the city were on the road to recovery, others were still scarred by years of hurricane damage. The moss that abundantly grew within the marshlands had begun its conquest over the city, creeping through the cracks of walls and overtaking many buildings due to floodwaters. Gray clouds cloaked the warehouse-infested city like a sheet of wool, keeping the dreary daydreamers in and the vibrant visionaries out. Its natives aimlessly roamed the streets with their eyes to the ground, keeping their heads out of the clouds and in their circumstances. It was a place of poverty, but we always managed to get by.

The air was rich with the faint rhythms of jazz and blues, which, if you listened carefully enough, was just what the doctor ordered to get you through the toughest of times. Little girls would play double Dutch in the streets, while the peppery aroma of Cajun spices gently wafted from the kitchens of homes where wives and mothers prepared family suppers. After a hard day's work, husbands and fathers would get together and play dominoes on porches, overseeing their children as they played in the streets without a care in the world. Life was very empty, very dull, very monotonous. No place at all for someone with a bright future indeed. That is, until now.

The Arts District was evolving. The urban wasteland of a city began to shed its battered shell. Those vibrant visionaries who once flourished on the outskirts of the city walls were now slowly but surely being drawn in like moths to a flame. An entirely new ecosystem was being born. World-class museums, extravagant art galleries, and five-star restaurants now occupied the plots where abandoned warehouses and properties once dwelled. From within these colorless walls emerged a beautiful and vibrant city, ready to spread its wings and soar toward a brighter future. The Butterfly of the South it soon was called. Who would have thought?

A thunderous roar bellowed from the menacing clock tower at the city center, omnipotent and overseeing—the city's warden whose shift never ended. The tower's foreboding cry resonated through every nook and cranny of the city, warning any unauthorized night crawlers to adhere to their midnight curfews and turn in before the nocturnal creatures of the Arts District became active and thrived.

However, tonight was no ordinary night. The cool air enveloped the city in a thin layer of dew. The lonely streets lay quiet and empty without a single trace of life, relieving the dimly lit lampposts of their duty of guiding weary travelers through the night. Only the gentle ticks and tocks of the grand clock tower and the melodic tunes of crickets' lullabies could be heard on this silent night.

Suddenly, a crescendo of pitter-pattering footsteps echoed through the alleys, disharmonizing the city's soothing symphony of ticks and tocks. His racing heart was unable to keep to the pace of the city's gentle metronome. Each breath was shorter than the last as he panted to the rhythm of the bursting drum within his chest. Beads of sweat rolled off of his brow like deflected raindrops on the windshield of a speeding car. His backpack clung to him for dear life as aerosol spray cans within it clanked and crackled, drowning out the melodic tunes of the crickets' lullabies. Who was this young boy out past curfew, painting the town? It was a boy by the name of Huey, twelve years of age and rather ordinary—the last person you would ever expect to have a bright future. He was a timid kid whose voice lacked confidence, often stumbling and stuttering with his words. He wore dingy Chuck Taylor sneakers, worn denim blue jeans, and a white, hooded sweatshirt that was as colorless and uninspired as a blank sheet of paper. He was rather ordinary indeed.

"I'm running out of time!" Huey desperately said to himself.

He clumsily reached into the pocket of his hooded sweatshirt without breaking stride, to check the time on his cell phone. It was already five minutes past midnight. A troublesome look overcame his face. He started to return the phone to his pocket, but it abruptly began to ring, and he dropped it in a startled panic. His heart sank into the pit of his stomach, where a swarm of butterflies had made their home. Terrified, his finger hovered over the green button with each second lasting longer than the last. His sweat formed into beads of ice on the nape of his neck as a ghastly chill went down his spine.

"H-hello?" Huey answered.

"You're late! Did you do your final task?"

The boy stood speechless. He clutched the phone to the side of his face as his lips began to quiver, making his breathing irregular.

"I-I'm sorry," Huey responded. "I-I just need a little more t-time."

"We don't do lateness!" the caller snapped. "I knew you weren't cut out for this!"

The boy's heart stopped, and his eyes widened. The caller's antagonizing words began to echo in his head.

"I-I'm so sorry!" Huey pleaded. "I won't let you guys down ever again—I promise! Please just give me another chance."

An uncomfortable silence filled the air as neither the boy nor the caller spoke. It was as if time itself was standing by, eagerly waiting for the silent deadlock between the two to come to an end.

"This is your last chance," the caller said. "If you have what it takes to be a T3, then prove us wrong. Call me when you've done the task."

The caller abruptly hung up. A rush of relief flooded through the boy's body. The ticks and tocks of the grand clock tower and the melodic tunes of crickets' lullabies returned to the night air. The boy released a heavy sigh as his shoulders collapsed and his damp palms unclenched. His moment of peace was short-lived as he quickly realized that he still had a ways to go to reach his destination. The boy pressed onward through the alleys and throughways with the pitter-pattering of his footsteps, the clanking and crackling of aerosol spray cans, and the air of a second wind.

At last, the boy arrived at a large warehouse at 121 Painters Street. Painters Street was once a run-down neighborhood, infamous for its crime and violence. It was a neighborhood of colorless people with uninspired dreams. Swindlers, thieves, vandals, two-timers, you name it. Only the lowest of the low would dare hang out there. It was a rough place to live, to say the least. That is, until now.

The entire neighborhood was being renovated and restored. The foreclosed apartments had been transformed into a marvelous shopping strip, home to all of the finer things of high society—designer retail stores, exquisite restaurants, local entertainment. Only the classiest of the classy could shop here. No place for lowlifes.

As the boy approached the side of the warehouse, he pulled out his phone and scrolled through it to review an old message.

"Your final task: tag your signature on the warehouse at 121 Painters Street as the newest member of the Two-Toned-Taggerz," the message read.

The Two-Toned-Taggerz, the T3s for short, was a mischievous group of youths who had made quite a name for themselves within the Arts District. Petty thefts, disorderly conduct, vandalism—no rule was too tough for them to break. They lived by the rules of the streets, rule number one being that there were no rules, of course. They believed that there were only two types of people in this world: winners and losers, those who take and those who are taken from. You were either with them or against them. This was what they knew to be true of the world. It was as simple as black and white, their signature colors. Lawless freedom, streets to call home, and a family of their own—this group of misfits had it all.

The boy returned the phone to his pocket and took a knee at the large sidewall of the warehouse. He carefully reached over his shoulder to remove his backpack, unzipping it to reveal the aerosol spray cans within.

"Time to get to work," Huey said to himself.

The hissing and crackling of aerosol spray cans filled the air like a nest of rattlesnakes warding off any trespassing predators. Colorful waves of mist gracefully flowed from the boy's handheld can, following the instruction of his swaying arm as he conducted an orchestra of paint. It was as if the spray can was an extension of his body. His motions were fluid and precise as he exhibited complete control over every tiny particle of paint. It was like watching poetry in motion.

Several minutes went by, and the boy stepped back to wipe his brow and examine his work so far. He observed it intently with a discerning eye, looking for even the slightest mistake, until a peculiar sound caught his attention in the distance. The boy turned away from the wall and cautiously walked to the curb to determine the source of the sound. The faint sound seemed to be getting louder as he fixed his eyes to the end of the long strip that was Painters Street. The soft, steady tempo of the distant sound continued to pulsate and grow louder.

"*What is that sound?*" Huey softly said to himself.

As the boy squinted his eyes to peer into the distance, flashing red and blue lights entered into his line of sight. His eyes widened, and his jaw dropped as if the wind had snatched the very breath from his chest. The aerosol spray can escaped the grasps of his fingers and plummeted to the ground as he stood paralyzed in fear. The aluminum can crashed against the asphalt road, snapping him out of his daze. The boy hastily ran back to the wall to secure his belongings as to not leave behind a trace of his existence. The faint pulse of the distant sound had now grown into long, wailing cries, piercing through the silence of the night like a fired bullet through stilled water. The boy clumsily grabbed the aerosol spray cans with trembling hands and returned them to the opened backpack. The pounding of his fluttering heart synchronized with the impending sirens, intensifying with each passing moment. He slung his backpack over his shoulder and dashed down the nearest ally like a criminal fleeing from the scene of his crime. His heart raced, and his body went numb. His mind was void of any thoughts. Only the primal instinct of flight compelled his body to press onward. There was neither a sense of pain nor tiredness. There was only a desire to escape. The oppressing sirens engulfed the night air. The boy ignored the antagonizing beams of strobing lights along the alley walls in the corners of his eyes, afraid to look back.

"*Freeze!*" the officer howled from a distance.

The officer's command fell on deaf ears; the boy did not skip a single beat in his stride. With each twist and turn through the alleyways, the boy's hopelessness grew, unable to escape the sirens and flashing lights. His breathing shortened as the walls began closing in, making the oxygen in the air scarcer by the second. His phone suddenly rang, releasing him from his trance.

"Incoming call from Ash," the phone screen read.

His heart sank. He realized that he never called to report his task being completed.

Should I answer? Huey thought. *This was my last chance. What should I do?*

The boy reluctantly moved his finger to calm the persistent ringing of the phone, unprepared for what was to come of the impending conversation. Just as his finger clicked to answer the incoming call, a great, white light blinded him. Disoriented and afraid, he crashed into a solid figure before him, sending him tumbling to the ground like a discarded rag doll. He felt the coolness and hardness of the pavement pressed against his face and the palm of his hand as he looked to his cracked phone that lay just within his reach. It emitted a faint voice that was drowned out in a sea of static as it began to slowly fade between life and death. As the boy slowly reached to respond to the caller, its last spark of life dwindled away, and the shattered screen faded to black as if the ending credits to a feature-length film had just come to a close. The boy instead deterred his reach to a photograph that lay next to the broken phone. Tears began to fill his eyes as he pulled the photograph toward him, returning it to his pocket.

"You have the right to remain silent. Anything you say can and will be used against you in a court of law ..."

The boy quietly lay there as the officer read him his rights, as if he were just another common, colorless criminal.

"You have the right to an attorney. If you cannot afford an attorney, one will be provided for you ..."

As the officer continued to recite his scripted speech, the boy's consciousness began to fade as he ceased to hear any more sounds. The flashing lights began to nullify as the world around him faded into nothingness. There was neither a sound nor a single light of hope. There was only darkness, emptiness, and regret.

Chapter 2
If You Can't Do the Time

Punishment is justice for the unjust.
—SAINT AUGUSTINE

"How many times are we going to go through this?" Officer Bluebell said with frustration in his voice. "I can't keep arresting you and letting you off with a slap on the wrist, Huey."

The officer rested his burly arms on the cool, metal table. He tapped his thick fingers on the table's surface as he looked upon the boy with restless eyes. The boy sat quietly at the other end of the table with slouched shoulders and folded arms, keeping the overbearing presence of the officer at a distance. His eyes shifted toward the floor, remaining unresponsive to the officer's inquiries.

"Have you been keeping up in school?" Officer Bluebell went on. "I thought you were considering joining a school team? Or what about that afterschool part-time job down at the civic center? Did you ever look into that?"

The boy remained silent and continued to avoid making eye contact. The officer removed his hat and placed it on the table in front of him. He began running his coarse hands over his face as if lathering it with cold water. He leaned back in his chair and released a heavy sigh as he continued to examine the unresponsive boy. The soft, mid-morning light crept through the cracks of the blinds, entering into the solemn atmosphere of the room. The cheerful chirping of birds could be heard from outside the window as they attempted to soothe the tension within the gloomy holding room.

"Come on, Huey, what's it going to take for me to get through to you?" Officer Bluebell asked now with concern in his voice. "I know you're better than this."

The officer paused to read the boy's body language. A look of disgust came to the tight-lipped boy's face as his eyes rose to meet those of the officer's. His pursed lips loosened and began to crinkle. The officer leaned forward in anticipation of the long-awaited response.

"What do *you* know?" Huey sneered.

The officer slowly folded back into his seat, stunned with disbelief by the boy's words. He took a heavy breath to compose himself before speaking.

"What do I know?" Officer Bluebell solemnly said. "I know it's been tough for you ... ever since the day ..."

Silence once again filled the room. Even the chirping birds outside the window brought their pleasant chatter to a close. The air became thick and dense with tension as the stalemate of their unwavering stares endured through the silence. Eventually, the boy surrendered, returning his glossy gaze to the floor. The officer noticed the change in the boy's eyes.

"You were still so young," Officer Bluebell continued. "Moving from foster home to foster home, fending for yourself, having nowhere to call home. I can only imagine how it must have been for you."

The boy remained unshaken.

"You're a good kid," Officer Bluebell softly said. "I know you are. And I know that you're better than this, Huey. I know how lost and afraid you must feel, but hanging around with that gang of hoodlums isn't the answer."

"Well that 'gang of hoodlums' is all I have!" Huey shouted with a cracked voice.

The officer looked upon the boy with sympathetic eyes. The boy's once cool and calm demeanor was no more. His breaths became panted and irregular as the thick, tensioned air flowed in and out of his flaring nostrils. His eyes glowed with a pinkish hue, fighting back impending tears like two levees ready to rupture under the pressure of hurricane floodwaters. The officer closed his eyes and slowed his breathing, realizing that he could not let his personal tie to the boy compromise his judgment as an impartial party. He had a duty to uphold, after all.

"Listen, I've done everything I can to keep you out of trouble, but you're not leaving me with any more options," Officer Bluebell asserted. "I'm an officer of the law, and it's my duty to serve and protect, which means I can't keep covering for you, Huey. Either things have to change or I'll be forced to treat you like I would any other delinquent that comes through here. So what's it going to be?"

A familiar silence filled the room. It was as if the entire world had stopped spinning in anticipation of the boy's final verdict. Moments later, the boy calmed his breathing and seemed to find a new resolve.

"Whatever …" Huey murmured.

The officer shook his head in disappointment. He reached for his hat on the table and carefully adjusted it back on his head, releasing another heavy sigh. He pinched the bridge of his nose and began caressing the corners of his shut eyes.

"If that's how it is, then you leave me with no other choice," Officer Bluebell said. "We're going to have to send you to—"

A sudden knock at the door interrupted the two, cutting the officer's words short. A woman abruptly opened the door and entered the room. She was a fellow officer in her midthirties it would seem. The boy remembered seeing her seated at the receptionist's desk earlier that morning as he was brought into the police department.

"Bluebell!" the female officer barked. "There's someone here to speak with you."

"I'll be there in a moment," Officer Bluebell responded.

The officer returned his attention to the boy.

"I'll finish dealing with you after I tend to our surprise guest," Officer Bluebell unenthusiastically said.

The boy was left alone as the two officers made their exit. The door slammed upon their departure, sending harsh echoes through the lonely, empty room. The boy glared at his reflection in the one-way mirror with resentful eyes, like a caged zoo animal scowling at unseen spectators. He sat there in silence, accompanied only by the taunting ticks and tocks of the clock hanging above the entryway of the room. The boy stared at the clock as he fidgeted in his chair. The relentless ticks and tocks became more menacing with each passing second. Several minutes passed as the boy's anxiety grew. He looked down to his lap and moved his hand toward the pocket of his hooded sweatshirt. He began to carefully pull something out. It was the photograph from before. Just as the photograph was fully removed from his pocket, the room door swung back open. The boy hastily concealed the photograph as the officer returned. However, he was not alone. A tall, slender, and rather stylish man accompanied him. He wore a paisley-patterned shirt of many colors with an unbuttoned collar that elegantly flowed with his every motion, no matter how slight, as if he carried with him a personal ocean breeze. His shirt was neatly tucked into his smooth, suede pants whose hems just barely kissed the top of his casual yet crisp loafers, which he wore without socks, of course. Atop his head, a suave, fedora-styled hat futilely contained a sea of kinky-textured curls that naturally flowed out from under the hat's brim. His glinting eyes peaked over the horizons of his dark, circular sunglasses like two partially eclipsed crescent moons. He was rather stylish indeed.

"So you're the young graffiti artist?" the tall, slender man kindly questioned.

"Who wants to know?" Huey rudely responded.

The man took a step back and chuckled, much to the boy's surprise. The boy sensed that there was something different about him.

"You're absolutely right!" the man said. "Where are my manners? My name is Anthony Pastel, but you can just call me Pastel for short, if you'd like. I'm a traveling artist and the owner of the new gallery at 121 Painters Street."

A shocked expression overcame the boy's face. He had no idea that anyone, and an artist at that, owned the once abandoned warehouse at 121 Painters Street. The boy remained speechless as man continued.

"And according to the signature on the side of my building," Pastel continued, "you must be Huey. It's a pleasure to meet you."

The man extended his hand to the boy. The puzzled boy fixated his eyes on the man's paint-stained hand, still in shock at the revelation of the man's identity.

"You'd be smart to show a little respect and shake Mr. Pastel's hand," Officer Bluebell interjected. "After all, he's the reason you're not being sent to the Juvenile Detention center."

The boy's attention averted to the officer with widened eyes and an opened mouth. The boy's puzzled expression turned into one of dread upon learning what his fate would have been. He meagerly turned his attention back to the tall, slender man.

"You're a very talented artist, Huey," Pastel sincerely said. "Though you're a little rough around the edges. Your style is crude and unrefined. It lacks ... soul. I think with a little guidance, you could really inspire people through your art. You just need someone to teach you."

The boy's face returned to a state of bewilderment. His gaze bounced back and forth between the officer and the tall, slender man. He observed the two men intently, as if waiting for one of them to make a sudden move. Just as the boy fixed his mouth to speak, the officer placed his coarse hand on his shoulder.

"We're going to try something different this time," Officer Bluebell declared. "Instead of sending you away as originally planned, starting tomorrow you'll be serving as Anthony's apprentice."

"It will be an honor to work alongside you, Huey," Pastel said with an earnest smile. "I look forward to seeing what magnificent things we will create together!"

The boy remained frozen in his seat as if his body were turned to stone by Medusa's glaring gaze. Sitting there, stiff as a statue, was all the boy could do as his destiny was placed into the hands of the man named Pastel. The boy finally gathered the strength to make one last, voluntary action of his body in the form of a feeble and defeated sigh.

"Perhaps you'll learn to put your vandalism to good use," Officer Bluebell said with a snicker. "Like we always say: don't do the crime if you can't do the time!"

Chapter 3
Different Strokes

Art enables us to find ourselves and
lose ourselves at the same time.
-THOMAS MERTON

"I welcome you to Spirit Rise!" Pastel shouted with outstretched arms.

The boy stared at the tall, slender man with uninspired eyes as the two stood at the entrance of the gallery at 121 Painters Street. It was noon. The man self-consciously lowered his outstretched arms in response to the boy's lack of enthusiasm. He motioned his loosely closed fist to his mouth and cleared his throat with an assertive grunt, alleviating the awkwardness of the moment as he turned his attention to the locked entrance door. He clumsily patted himself down in search of his keys as they rested tightly tucked within the back pocket of his smooth, suede pants. The last place he thought to check, of course.

"You're a pretty lucky fellow, you know?" Pastel said with a sly grin. "The gallery's official opening isn't until next week. You'll be the first to lay your eyes on my magnificent collection!"

The man finally got the front door of the gallery to open after several seconds of fumbling the keys. The boy was hesitant to follow him into the dark, shadowy building.

"Come on in!" a zealous voice echoed out of the darkness. "Don't be shy!"

The boy took a large gulp and took a slow, reluctant stride into the dark, empty mouth of the beast that dwelled at 121 Painters Street. His heart began to pound as the butterflies in his stomach swarmed, until the click of a light switch calmed his nerves. As light pried its way through the cracks of the boy's shut lids, he carefully peaked one eye open to find himself standing in a bright, open room with artwork all around. Statues and sculptures, potteries and paintings, you name it. There were even things the boy could not describe.

"So what do you think?" Pastel asked. "Truly magnificent, no?"

The boy stood there speechless, in awe.

"Since this is your first day, we'll start off with a tour of the gallery so that you can learn your way around," Pastel said with a smile. "After all, it's quite easy to get lost in the art, as I'm sure you'll come to find out. Shall we begin?"

The tall, slender man walked toward an entryway that led to a walled-off section of the gallery, gesturing for the boy to follow. The boy faintheartedly followed suit; his curiosity had gotten the better of him. The man led the boy through the neatly filed hallways decked with fine art. The boy could not keep his eyes from wondering from side to side as he examined all of the different painted pieces.

"Every work of art is unique in its own way," Pastel righteously exalted. "Each having its very own story to share with the world, and at the heart of each work lays the soul of its artist through which its story is communicated."

The man abruptly stopped midstride as the distracted boy clumsily crashed into him from behind. The boy gathered himself and began to apologize until he noticed the tall, slender man stroking his chin with a stern look on his face.

"Hmm … I think it would be appropriate to give you a brief art history lesson first," Pastel declared. "We'll get you grounded in history before we get into my more contemporary collection!"

The two were stopped in front of a large painting at the end of the hall depicting several people relaxing in the shade in a park.

A Sunday Afternoon on the Island of La Grande Jatte
(Georges Seurat, 1884–1886)

"Ahh! *A Sunday Afternoon on the Island of La Grande Jatte*, 1884!" Pastel exclaimed. "One of Georges Seurat's most famous works and an excellent example of a style known as Pointillism! This is a style of painting that creates one unified image by contrasting several small dots or brushstrokes of color. What a magnificent visual experience. Do you not agree, Huey?"

The boy stared upon the painting with squinted eyes. His attention was drawn to a little girl dressed in white who appeared to be staring back at him.

"Why is the little girl the only one not in shade?" Huey asked. "And why isn't she looking with everyone else?"

"Magnificent questions!" Pastel cheered. "There are many secrets behind several famous works that only their creators know. Perhaps you will be the one to unravel their mysteries one day!"

The tall, slender man laughed with delight. He tapped the boy on the shoulder and began to walk back down the hall from where they came. A peculiar feeling overcame the boy as he took one last look into the eyes of the little girl dressed in white. The tall, slender man called out to him to hurry along as the two made their way to the next painting down an adjacent hallway.

"Another one of my favorites!" Pastel rejoiced. "Vincent van Gogh's *The Starry Night*, 1889."

The Starry Night (Vincent van Gogh, 1889)

The two now stood in front of a painting depicting a view of a beautifully starlit night. The boy gazed upon the painting with wonder.

"Although this painting depicts a nighttime scene, van Gogh actually painted it from memory during the daytime," Pastel explained. "It's a depiction of Saint-Rémy-de-Provence in France outside his window. A magnificent Post-Impressionist oil painting of a beautiful night landscape!"

The boy could not look away from the entrancing painting. Its splendid brush strokes captured his imagination. The twinkle in his eye gleamed just as brightly as the enchanting stars within the painting's deep and dark sky. The tall, slender man smiled at the boy, delighted by the boy's entrapment of the piece.

"Let us move on, shall we?" Pastel softly said. "I'm sure the stars will not go anywhere!"

Pastel nudged the boy to keep moving forward, breaking him from his trance. The two continued to traverse through Spirit Rise's cornfield of hallways. Moments later, they came to another stop.

"Hmm … now this is an interesting piece worth mention," Pastel grimly said. "*The Scream* by Expressionist artist Edvard Munch, 1893."

The Scream (Edvard Munch, 1893)

The boy turned his attention to a strange painting of a rather agonized man standing on a winding hill road. He was overcome by an eerie sensation as he peered into the ominous, blood-orange sky of *The Scream*.

"I don't like this one," Huey said with uneasiness in his voice.

Pastel looked at the boy and released a nervous chuckle.

"I will admit that this piece is a tad unsettling," he said with an apprehensive smile. "Nevertheless, this painting has become rather popular. It has even been called an icon of modern art, a *Mona Lisa* for its time.[1] Let us just be glad that we are not the poor fellow in the painting!"

The boy was not amused by the painting or by Pastel's attempt to lighten the mood. He continued to look at the painting, frozen by an unshakable feeling of fear. Pastel observed the boy's haunted face and swiftly nudged him to keep moving onward.

"Speaking of," Pastel said. "Our next pit stop will surely impress!"

His face lit up with excitement in anticipation of their next destination. The boy hastily followed behind him. A chill went down his spine as he glanced over his shoulder to take one last look at the unnerving painting. The two made their way toward the farthest hall within the gallery. Just as they were about to stop for the fourth time, Pastel placed his hands over the boy's eyes.

"Are you ready for the grand finale?" Pastel asked.

He carefully guided each of the boy's uncertain steps down the final stretch toward their destination.

"Voilà!" Pastel shouted. "The crème de la crème! The pièce de résistance! The moment you have been waiting for!"

Pastel hastily uncovered the boy's eyes. The boy blinked several times to readjust his blurred vision. As his vision cleared, he looked up to see a painting of a rather elegant woman. He glared at the painting intently as he began to feel a sense of familiarity. He honed his attention to the enigmatic smile of the woman as he tried to remember where he had seen her before. Pastel looked upon the boy with astonishment, as the boy had yet to figure out the identity of the painting.

"You still do not recognize this piece?" Pastel gasped with disbelief. "Why, this is the best known, the most visited, the most written about, the most sung about, the most parodied work of art in the world!"[2]

The boy looked at Pastel with a face as blank as a slate. Pastel released a surrendering sigh.

"This is Leonardo da Vinci's, and perhaps history's, most magnificent work of art!" Pastel exalted. "The *Mona Lisa*. Surely that name rings a bell, no?"

Mona Lisa (Leonardo da Vinci, 1503–1517)

A thoughtful look came to the boy's face as he continued to contemplate the painting. A large vein began twitching in Pastel's forehead. It took everything in his power to remain calm as the boy's lack of appreciation for the art world's greatest treasure continued. A jolt of inspiration finally sparked the boy to recall something.

"Oh yeah ..." Huey casually said. "I think I've heard of this one before."

Pastel dropped his head into his open-palmed hand. He then slowly wiped his hand down the length of his face, as if wiping the criticism off of it. He took a long, deep inhale of air through his nose, followed by a heavy exhale through his mouth.

"Yes, I'm sure you've heard of the *Mona Lisa* somewhere before," Pastel said. "The portrait of the woman is believed to have been painted sometime in the very early 1500s."

"Wow!" Huey said. "That's how old this thing is?"

"That is correct!" Pastel boasted. "You are looking at another original. You cannot imagine what it took for me to get my hands on this masterpiece!"

The boy marveled at the painting with a newfound appreciation for its majesty. It was not every day that one got the opportunity to stand before the *Mona Lisa,* after all. His attention once again returned to the uncertain expression on the elegant woman's face. He remained perplexed by her enigmatic smile.

"Why is she smiling?" Huey asked.

"Another magnificent question!" Pastel affirmed. "Unfortunately, I do not have the answer. No one knows for sure what the cause of her faint and ever so famous smile is. It is perhaps the biggest mystery within the art world."

Several minutes went by as the two gawked at the painting with slacked jaws as if they were both witnessing it for the very first time. Pastel reached into the pocket of his pants to reveal an antiquated pocket watch. He carefully clicked the thumbnail opening, and its unpolished case slowly swung open on its rusty hinge.

* * * 1:35 p.m. * * *

"Oh my," Pastel murmured. "It would appear that we have let time get the better of us. We will have to conclude the tour for today. Come along, Huey. Let us move on to the hands-on portion of the day."

The boy cocked his head to the side with a brooding face, unaware of what Pastel had in store for him. Pastel clapped his hands twice, signaling the boy to follow as he made his way toward a winding staircase that led down into the basement of the gallery. The boy scurried behind him into the depths of Spirit Rise, charged with adrenaline for what awaited them in the dark dungeon. As the two arrived at the base of the winding staircase, Pastel flicked another light switch to illuminate the room. The wide-eyed boy scanned the large, open room in awe. The stockpiled oasis was filled with a vast array of artistic tools and crafts. Oil paints, watercolors, pastels, you name it. Any art supply or utensil that any artist could ever dream of was all right there. There was even an entire color spectrum of aerosol spray cans neatly arranged on an elongated shelf that stretch around the perimeter of the room in more colors and hues than the boy could have ever imagined. It was as if the Greek goddess Iris herself had plucked a rainbow right out of the very sky and lined the walls of the room with it. Several sketchbooks were scattered across the room on the tabletops and the floor, while paint-daubed canvases, both big and small, roosted on elevated, wooden easels like regal birds. It was a Garden of Eden for art—the place where art began. It was truly an artists' haven.

"Welcome to my artist sanctuary!" Pastel roared with gusto. "This studio is where I create works for my personal collection. From henceforth, all that you see here is at your disposal. Let us embark on a journey through the magnificent world of art together!"

Sensation was written all over the boy's face as he remained paralyzed with bliss. The wonderland of possibilities was almost too much for him to take in. He snapped out of his dreamlike daze as Pastel dangled a rather colorless and uninspired-looking paintbrush in the peripheral of his vision.

"But before we get to the good stuff, you must first learn the basics," Pastel said with a sly grin. "You must learn how to walk before I can teach you to run. Shall we begin?"

Hours went by as Pastel taught the boy the fundamentals of traditional painting. He taught the boy how to hold the brush properly, where to place his hands, and even the proper sitting posture. There was an entire art behind how to go about creating art. Who would have thought?

"All right then!" Pastel cried with relief. "I think you're ready to create your first masterpiece! Although … deciding on the subject matter is often half the battle. Huey, is there anything in particular that you would like to paint?"

The boy scratched his head and scrunched his eyebrows. He began to mumble to himself as he parsed through his memories like a pirate searching for a hidden treasure trove of thoughts. Pastel looked upon the furrow-browed boy amusingly as he strained so passionately to think of something.

"What about that photograph you were fumbling with in your pocket the other day?" Pastel suggested. "It seems to be rather important to you. Perhaps it can serve as a source of inspiration."

Silence suddenly disharmonized the room. Huey's face sank like a dense stone thrown into a crystal-clear pond. The boy sat there motionless and silent.

"Is something the matter, Huey?" Pastel asked with concern in his voice.

The boy did not respond.

"Is there something that I said that troubled you? Please tell me what it was that I said."

"This is stupid," Huey said. "I don't feel like painting anymore."

The boy loosened his grip and released the paintbrush from his hand, sending it plummeting to the floor below. Pastel looked upon the boy with discouraged eyes. He carefully picked up the paintbrush at the boy's feet and gently bobbed its soiled bristles in a cup, making murky the cup's once clear water. The attention of his eyes never once left the boy across the table.

"If you prefer not to talk about what's troubling you, then perhaps you would prefer to paint about it," Pastel suggested. "That is what art is all about, after all. Speaking from the soul."

He offered the paintbrush back to the boy, who aggressively slapped it out of Pastel's hand, returning it to the floor.

"I said I don't want to paint anymore!" Huey shrieked.

Pastel continued to look upon the huffing and puffing boy with discouraged eyes. He removed his dark, circular sunglasses, placing them into the pocket of his paisley-patterned shirt of many colors. Again, he reached into the pocket of his pants to reveal the antiquated pocket watch. He carefully clicked the thumbnail opening, swinging its unpolished case slowly open on its rusty hinge, and examined the clock's face.

"I believe this is all the time we have for today," Pastel asserted. "We will pick up tomorrow where we left off. You are free to leave if you would like."

Another dismal moment of silence filled the room as neither the boy nor Pastel budged an inch. The friction between the two was so intense that the rising temperature of the air could be felt on the skin. Finally, the boy snapped up from his chair and made his way toward the winding staircase that led back to the gallery's entrance level. Pastel calmly followed after the boy to escort him out. As they reached the front display room at the gallery's entrance, Pastel stopped short, as the boy no longer needed his guidance. Huey grabbed the doorknob and forcefully turned it to make his exit.

"Huey," Pastel gently called out.

The boy paused.

"Everyone is a work of art," Pastel continued. "Even the *Mona Lisa* was once a blank canvas, which means that we are all just masterpieces waiting to be painted. Even you. Always remember that."

The boy stood still with his hand fastened to the doorknob. The friction in the air dissipated as a gentle breeze of cool air flowed through the building's ventilating veins. The soothing moment of hesitation was short-lived as the boy proceeded to calmly walk out the door in silence.

Chapter 4

Birds of a Feather

The man who has no imagination has no wings.
-MUHAMMAD ALI

The city came back to life as the menacing clock tower struck the hour of five and husbands and fathers made their way home from a hard day's work, navigating through the hustle and bustle of the city's rush hour. The warm, late-afternoon air roared with booming and blaring horns as large, metal giants sluggishly crept through gridlock traffic like a herd of restless wildebeests roaming the savanna plains. The urban uproar persisted for hours, pouring into the early evening. The dimly lit lampposts awoke from their slumber and prepared for the nightshift as the sun began to set and clock out for the day. The boy walked the lonely sidewalks as the lively city began to settle. He dragged his lethargic feet across the hard cement, aimlessly roaming the streets with his eyes to the ground. The peppery aroma of Cajun spices gently wafted on the wind as wives and mothers and husbands and fathers and sons and daughters settled at family dinner tables. The boy kept his eyes fixed to the ground and away from the open windows of family-filled homes as their laughter and cheer spilled into the street. They seemed so peaceful, so loving, so happy. No place for someone with a troubled past. Or perhaps, maybe it was.

"Hey—yo, Huey!" A voice called from the distance.

The boy's head snapped up. His heart stopped, and his eyes widened as the familiar voice resonated in his ears. His shaking hands began to go numb as his lips began to quiver. He slowly turned his head over his shoulder toward the end of the street. The grinding growl of skateboard wheels washed out the laughter and cheer of family dinners. The boy shyly turned around as three older boys rapidly approached, drifting and gliding on the ocean of asphalt like three weaving electric eels.

"Found you!" Coal sneered with a sinister grin.

"Humph!" Greyson coldly scorned. "It's been a real chore hunting you down."

"Now, now let's not go jumping to conclusions," Ash sternly interjected. "Let's give our newest brother a chance to explain himself."

Ash was the leader of the notorious T3s. Unlike the rest of this colorless city with uninspired dreams, Ash had a bright future indeed. "The entire Arts District will know your name after I'm done with you!" he'd always promise his followers, and they believed him. He had a way with words. He gave you hope. He made you believe in a brighter future. He made you feel like family. If only his aerosol spray can were as big as his ambition, he would surely tag the entire world black and white if he could. The sky began to darken as the boy timidly shared the events of the past few days as they happened, not missing a single detail. The three older boys listened intently, astounded by the boy's misadventures with the officer and the tall, slender man.

"Whoa! That's unreal!" Coal shouted. "Ash said he heard 5-0 sirens in the background when he called you the other night. We thought you were a goner!"

"Yeah," Greyson scorned. "Breaking you out of jail would've been a real chore."

As the two older boys continued to bombard the boy with questions, the leader stepped forward, cutting them off.

"You didn't go and snitch on us did you?" Ash asked.

"N-no!" Huey meekly stuttered. "I-I would never say anything about you guys to the cops."

The boy began to shudder under the leader as his domineering presence overwhelmed that of the boy's. He shriveled under the pressure of the leader's truth-seeking glare, futilely attempting to stand his ground.

"I believe you," Ash lightheartedly asserted. "You're a brother now, after all."

The leader firmly gripped the shuddering shoulder of the boy, who instinctively shut his eyes. His shoulders jerked into a shrugged position, flinching in anticipation of the impending blow, like a startled tortoise withdrawing into the protection of its shell. A brief moment went by as the boy soon realized that he had not been struck. He carefully peered through his squinted eyes to discover a jovial expression on the leader's face. He was being embraced, not punished.

"That dirty cop has a lot of nerve messing with our brother Huey here!" Coal growled. "And who does this art guy think he is? He needs to be taught a lesson!"

The leader began pacing back and forth with crossed arms and a furrowed brow as the other three boys sat on pins and needles, watching his every movement. The face of the leader suddenly lit up with a mischievous grin.

"I think we should pay Huey's new buddy down at 121 Painters Street a visit tonight. You know, officially welcome him to the neighborhood. After all, since we're going to run this place one day, it's only right that we give him a warm T3 welcome!"

A discomforting look came to the boy's face as the two older boys leapt with joy over the leader's plan for revenge. A pit of despair developed in the boy's stomach as it began twisting and turning out of guilt. Even though they had their differences, the boy had grown rather fond of the tall, slender man. He wanted nothing more than to rightfully stand up for his teacher, but no words came out of his mouth. His muted vocal cords stripped his words of their power, causing them to shyly roll off his tongue and silently drift into the wind unheard. The three older boys were his brothers. His family. He could not let them down.

"Then it's settled," Ash proclaimed. "It goes down at midnight!"

* * * 12:00 a.m. Friday * * *

The menacing clock tower bellowed its thunderous midnight roar, warning all unauthorized creatures of the city to adhere to their curfews. However, tonight was no ordinary night, as four young boys defied its foreboding cry. The alleys and throughways reverberated with the grinding growl of skateboard wheels and the clanking and crackling of aerosol spray cans. Tonight would prove to be no ordinary night indeed. The four young boys arrived at the large warehouse at 121 Painters Street, where Spirit Rise now dwelled. The searching glow of a full moon aided in the clock tower's shift, monitoring the streets below from a bed of dark, low-hanging clouds. The thick and humid midnight air carried with it the faint, sweet scent of a distant rain. A storm was approaching.

"This place is huge!" Coal shouted. "How the heck are we supposed to get in this joint?"

"It's going to be a real chore from the looks of it," Greyson scorned.

The leader turned his attention to the boy. He noticed the anxious demeanor of the boy as he stood off to the side and away from the group.

"Huey," Ash called. "Any idea how to get in?"

The boy tensed up as the three older boys turned their attention to him. He could feel the burn of the persecuting stares of six answer-seeking eyes honed on his skin like magnifying glasses held to the sun. The boy began to crumble and fold like a dry, summer leaf futilely attempting to shield itself from the intense heat. He looked up to the behemoth of a building and began to reminisce about his time with the tall, slender man and all of the wonderful things he saw that day. He also thought about how kind and generous the man was to open up his entire studio to someone like him. Surely the boy would not double-cross the one who saved him from Juvenile Jail for this band of bandits he called brothers. Or perhaps, for the closest thing to a family he had.

"W-well," Huey muttered, "there's a small basement window in the back … I th-think I might be able to fit through it and open the front door from inside."

A mischievous grin returned to the face of the leader as he looked upon the timid boy. He began to chuckle, grabbing the boy by the shoulder.

"That-a-boy, Huey!" Ash boasted. "You've really come into your own. You're truly worthy to call yourself a T3."

The boy could not believe what he had just heard. The corners of his mouth softly rose into a modest smile as his eyes dazzled. He had never felt such affection from someone whom he had admired so. The leader's words of affirmation touched the boy's heart and resonated in his soul like nothing he had ever experienced before. For the very first time in his life, the boy felt as though he was useful. That he was needed. That he was not worthless after all.

"So here's the game plan," Ash declared. "We'll wait here until Huey lets us in through the front door from the inside."

The two older boys applauded and cheered as their fearless leader rallied the troops for their covert mission of mischief. Even the boy could not help but be eager as the leader revealed the details of the plan.

"And once inside," Ash continued, "we'll show this guy what real art looks like!"

The three older boys removed aerosol spray cans in both black and white from their backpacks. The eagerness on the boy's face immediately washed away. They planned on tagging the inside of the gallery. The boy went into a silent panic as his breathing shortened and his heart started pounding. A black tar pit of fear consumed his imagination as he began to envision all of the wonderful works of Spirit Rise sinking into a dark, muddy abyss one by one. The boy desperately reached out for the only remaining piece as it barely escaped the grasp of his fingertips. His hand feebly lowered as he watched the *Mona Lisa* fully submerge and plummet to the depths of the tar. He was powerless to save them.

"Huey, snap out of it!" Coal shouted.

The boy was startled back to reality. His frantic breathing gradually slowed to a steady pace as his heart returned to a gentler rhythm. He reluctantly proceeded to make his way around the perimeter of the building as the three older boys cheered him on from a distance. He weighed his options in his head, trying to find some way out from between the rock and the hard place he had put himself. His time quickly ran out as he arrived at the small basement window.

If I do this, all of Mr. Pastel's art will be destroyed, Huey thought to himself. *But if I don't, I'll never be able to face the guys again.*

The boy crouched to his knee to slide open the small window. He carefully squeezed his body through the narrow slit feet-first, just barely fitting. He made a harsh crash landing on the floor of the dark and empty studio room, underestimating the drop. As he stood, doubt began to fill his mind. He soon realized that it was too late for second-guessing; the window from where he entered was no longer within his reach. The only way out now was through the front door. The boy made his way through the studio toward the winding staircase that led to the ground level of the gallery. Memories of the tall, slender man flooded his mind as he made his way upstairs and through the gallery. The boy cautiously crept through the hallways as the wooden floorboards creaked and groaned like lost souls, warning him to turn back with each step. Just as he prepared to round the final corner that led into the front display room, he stopped short. He realized that this was the end of the line and that moving beyond this point would bring his darkest fears to fruition. There was no turning back. He clenched his fists and took in a deep breath.

"You can do this," Huey whispered to himself. "Three, two, one!"

A faint echo of laughter slithered through the halls. The startled boy whipped his head over his shoulder at breakneck speed in response to the mysterious sound.

"H-hello?" Huey hesitantly asked. "Is someone th-there?"

There was no response. Only silence. The boy's heartbeat amplified. Paranoia began setting in as he became conscious of his breathing. He scouted through the darkness with chameleon eyes, sporadically bouncing his gaze from wall to wall. Mounted paintings followed him with watchful eyes as he aimlessly wandered back through the dark hallways. Several minutes passed as the boy began to think that he simply let his fear get the better of him. As he turned around to make his way back to the front, another echo of cackling laughter rolled through the halls. The boy was sure he had heard something this time.

"M-Mr. Pastel?" Huey frightfully called. "Is that y-you?"

Again, there was no response. The boy stood there with bated breath and icy veins as his blood began to run cold. His paranoia-induced senses heightened as he was no longer able to differentiate between reality and the tricks of his mind. He heard the delicate sound of something dripping on the floor. As the boy slowly turned his attention downward, he discovered a puddle of water at his feet that he had not noticed before. A puzzled expression came to his face as a pungent odor filled his nostrils. He kneeled down and gently placed the palm of his hand on the surface of the puddle. The water was thick and heavy. The boy drew his hand closer, carefully examining the mysterious liquid. Much to his surprise, he discovered that his hand was covered in paint. The questioning boy narrowed his vision as something inexplicable began to take place in the palm of his hand. His unblinking eyes refused to accept the sight as the paint came to life in his hand, taking the form of a rather vibrantly colored bird. The boy looked on, stunned, as the tiny bird frantically fluttered down the hall. Before the boy could even register what had just happened right before his eyes, he was thrown back on his rear as a flock of birds took flight from the paint puddle in a spiraling vortex of colorful feathers. The boy speechlessly watched as the flock of birds frenziedly stormed down the hall and around the corner. His body went numb. His legs grudgingly began pulling him forward as if they were possessed. His slow, creeping steps turned into hysterical strides as he pursued the flock of birds down the halls. As the panted boy rounded the final corner, he came across a dead-ended hallway with not a single trace of the birds in sight. The boy cautiously moved toward the end of the hall, carefully examining his surroundings. Finally, he arrived at the end of the dark hall. He looked up to see a familiar painting mounted on the wall before him. It was *A Sunday Afternoon on the Island of La Grande Jatte*. The boy recalled the painting from his tour as a troubled look came to his face. He could not shake the feeling that something was different about it. He leaned in closer to analyze the painting further.

"You appear to be lost, my dear child!" a mysterious voice said.

The boy drew back in alarm, keeping his eyes glued to the painting. A vile, ear-wrenching screech emitted from the painting, causing its surface to ripple and wave. The boy fell back on his rear, petrified with terror as a large, feathered creature emerged from within the painting.

The horrifying Harpy creature had the body of a majestic bird and the face of a human. Mounted paintings rocked and rattled as the creature flapped its mighty wings, shaking the walls with great gusts of wind. Its fierce, fish-scaled talons floated in the air like razor-sharp daggers primed for butchering as its long, elegant tail feathers swept along the floor. It stared at the boy with its observant owl eyes, recording every sweating pore on the boy's brow. The boy looked on in horror as the Harpy creature wrapped itself in its wings like a cocoon and began to shift and morph its body into the form of a ghastly man. His oil-paint skin smudged and smeared on his face like a muddy mask, dripping between the crevices of his wicked Cheshire-cat grin of perfectly sculpted, white marble teeth. Atop his head, a sophisticated, feather-crowned hat settled on a sea of long, dreadlocked strands of hair with paint-daubed tips that squirmed like snakes. Its mighty wings draped around his shoulders, creating a shawl of vibrantly colored feathers as long, elegant sashes made of smooth silk flowed from his torso. Different species of vibrantly colored parrots and birds of paradise swarmed and flocked around him as origami doves and cranes peacefully fluttered with paint-spattered paper wings, and the vibrantly colored parrots and birds-of-paradise decorated the walls and floor with their paint-dripping feathers. He gently drifted and wafted through the air like a dancing dragon as sweet-scented cherry blossom petals rained down from his garment, creating gentle ripples on the floor's surface. The gallery's floor transformed into a transparent, wooden pond as a school of Japanese koi serenely swam underneath him, illuminating the hall with the goldenrod glow of their shimmering scales.

"I shall help you find what you are looking for!" the ghastly man asserted with a wicked grin.

The boy remained paralyzed on the floor as the ghastly man summoned a large, blank canvas as a small, vibrantly colored bird began pecking at the boy's clothing, searching his pockets. As the boy wildly flailed his arms to rid himself of the bird's incessant pestering, he discovered that it had returned to the ghastly man with his photograph in its beak.

"My, my, what do we have here?" the man asked. "This shall do just fine!"

As the boy lunged forward to reclaim the photograph, the man began swabbing the large, blank canvas with the tips of his paint-daubed dreadlocks. The boy watched in astonishment as the man painted an exact replica portrait of the photograph.

"W-what's going on?" Huey asked. "Why are you doing this?"

As the photograph gently floated back to the boy, the man began to chuckle.

"Why, you ask? Because I have been summoned here to help you find what you have lost, my dear child. Remember this:

> "What you seek is within the heart—
> And there you will find the Lost Art."

A baffled expression came to the boy's face as everything in his surroundings was suddenly engulfed in a blinding, white light.

Chapter 5
Where the Sun Don't Shine

Anonymous

I wake to golden sunlit rays;
Exposed am I without the shade.
The piercing light distorts my gaze.
For darkness is where I once lay.
My eyes were opened to the truth.

The boy winced as the bright, piercing light pried its way into his tightly shut eyelids. He raised his hand to his brow as a visor to screen the intense light from his eyes. His vision was blurry, and his mind was dazed. He felt a sensation of heat envelop his skin as he mustered his strength to attempt to stand. He felt the gentle tickle of fresh-scented grass pressed against his hand as he propped himself in an upright seated position. He groggily rubbed his eyes, and as his vision cleared, he found himself to be in an open park lawn. He shielded his eyes and looked up to the sky to see the bright, burning sun overhead. The boy woozily rose to his feet, brushing off the blades of grass stuck to his clothing.

"Where am I?" Huey whispered to himself. "And how did I get here?"

His eyes panned across the open, outdoor landscape, looking for a familiar landmark, but he recognized nothing. Through the trees, a large body of water settled in the distance, and he could see the sails of boats.

"Where there are boats there must be people!" Huey convinced himself.

The boy ran through the park toward the large body of water in hopes to find someone that could tell him where he was. After making his way through the grove of trees, he arrived at a riverbank that seemed rather busy with activity. The boy sighed with relief as he saw all of the people and families relaxing in the shade, escaping from the heat of the bright, burning sun. He noticed two women sitting down peering off into the distance and casually approached them.

"Excuse me," Huey politely said. "Can you please tell me where I am?"

Neither of the two women responded.

"Um ... hello?" Huey awkwardly continued.

Still, the two women did not respond. The boy looked at the two women as they ignored his presence and continued to gaze off into the distance. He slowly backed away, annoyed at their rudeness. He then turned his attention to a man and woman standing together. The peculiar man wore a top hat and held a cane neatly tucked under the pit of his arm while the woman wore a long dress and held an umbrella, shielding them from the bright, burning sun's rays.

"Excuse me," Huey said. "I seem to have gotten lost somehow. Could you please tell me how I can get to 121 Painters Street from here?"

Neither the man nor the woman responded. The boy's eyebrow twitched with annoyance.

"Hey, I'm talking to you!" Huey impatiently shouted.

Both the man and the woman continued to ignore him as they gazed off into the distance. Again, the boy walked off grumbling, unable to understand the lack of manners of everyone he had encountered thus far. He stopped and began scanning the riverbank in search of someone who looked approachable.

Why isn't anyone talking to me? Huey thought.

As he looked around, he began to notice some rather bizarre sights. One woman to his right stood near the riverbank and appeared to be fishing. Her line loosely dangled in the shallow waters of the river's shore. No place for catching any fish. The boy looked back to his left to the man and the woman he had just spoken to and turned his attention to the woman's rather peculiar dog. Upon further examination, he discovered that it was not a dog but rather a monkey on a leash. A strange feeling overcame the boy's body as he became uncomfortable with his surroundings. He also noticed the strange attire of everyone, as men sported top hats and canes and old-fashioned pipes while women wore long dresses and held parasol umbrellas.

Why is everyone so overdressed? Huey thought. *It's got to be like eighty degrees out here.*

As the puzzled boy continued to examine the riverbank, his eyes met those of a little girl dressed in white. The boy shyly looked to each of his sides to confirm that the little girl dressed in white was in fact looking at him. She continued to peer at the boy with unblinking eyes as she softly raised her hand to wave.

"Hi!" the little girl sweetly shouted.

The boy took a gulp, cracked a nervous smile, and raised his hand to wave back to the little girl dressed in white.

"H-hello," Huey timidly responded.

The little girl seemed rather young. Too young to give the boy directions, but she was the only person to acknowledge him. The boy began to make his way toward her.

"E-excuse me," Huey said. "When I woke up, I was in this park. Could you possibly help me out? I'm not even sure what day it is."

The little girl dressed in white giggled.

"It's Sunday, silly!" she asserted. "It's always Sunday here!"

The boy was taken aback by her response. He studied her intently, looking for the slightest trace of insincerity on her face. Her innocent and genuine smile could tell no lies.

Sunday, Huey thought. *We were just at Spirit Rise early Friday morning. How could I have been asleep for that long? And what does she mean by 'It's always Sunday here'?*

As the boy paced while lost in thought, the little girl began tugging on his hooded sweatshirt, breaking his concentration.

"You don't look like you're from around here," the little girl said. "What's your name?"

"I guess I never introduced myself, did I?" Huey said while scratching his head. "My name is H … um …"

A confounded expression came to the boy's face as he realized that he could not remember his name. He slowly stepped away from the little girl dressed in white and walked to the shore of the riverbank. He peered into the water to see his reflection staring back at him as he tried to remember what he could of the night before. The little girl approached him from behind.

"Is something wrong?" she asked.

"N-no," the boy said. "I just must have bumped my head pretty hard the other night. I just need to get back home. By the way, why is everyone in the shade on such a nice, sunny day?"

The little girl giggled. She gently raised her hand in the air and pointed to the sun.

"Because it's always sunny here, silly! My mommy always says that I'll bake like a potato if I don't get in the shade, but I never listen!"

The boy looked at the little girl in shock as she made yet another statement that could not possibly be true.

"And where is 'here' exactly?" the boy asked.

"That's a silly question! La Grande Jatte of course!"

The boy looked at her in disbelief. He knew that La Grande Jatte was the name of the island in the painting in the gallery. The boy was convinced that she was simply playing with him. Realizing that he would get nothing out of this conversation with her, he turned his attention back to the river and began to wash his face in the water. The refreshing coolness relaxed his mind and calmed his nerves. The little girl gently sat down next to him and stared into the sky.

"Sometimes I wish it weren't always so sunny here," the little girl said. "My mommy says that there are places far, far away from here where the sun goes away and the shade covers everything! She says it's called nighttime. She says that at nighttime, the air gets cool, and the sky turns a deep and dark blue and is filled with tiny little suns called stars! I've never seen a starry night before, but my mommy always says this:

"Imagine a sky filled with stars—
Like freeing fireflies from jars."

The boy looked upon the little girl dressed in white as she sat there with a genuine smile. He was unsure of whether or not she was playing some sort of trick on him, but he could not help but smile back.

"Well I hate to brag," the boy boasted, "but where I come from, nighttime happens all the time! Maybe I can show you someday."

Her eyes lit up like two bright, burning stars in the night sky. She began jumping and cheering with delight as the boy rose to his feet to join her in celebration. After a few seconds of rejoicing, the little girl abruptly stopped. He looked at her with concerned eyes, noticing the serious expression that had come to her face.

"First thing first!" the little girl proclaimed. "We have to get you back if we want to see the nighttime sky!"

"You know how to get me back home?"

"Of course, silly! Follow me!"

A puzzled expression returned to the boy's face as she took him by the hand and pulled him back to the shore. The boy decided to play along, as she seemed certain of what she was talking about. She instructed him to crouch down on his hands and knees and look closely at the water's surface.

"Are you ready?" the little girl asked.

The boy snickered with amusement. He could not believe that he had played along with her game of Make-Believe for this long.

"Ready!" the boy eagerly shouted.

"All right!" the little girl hollered. "Three, two, one … off you go!"

The boy frantically flailed as the little girl shoved his head into the river. He could not believe what she had done. He panicked as he began to feel the sensation of drowning and his mouth filled with water. His body involuntarily forced him to hold his breath in vain as too much water had already entered into his lungs. The suffocating water rushed in, filling every internal nook and cranny, squeezing all of the oxygen out of his body. Distant memories began playing back in his mind like a projector slide show of old photos as he slipped in and out of consciousness. His vision blurred, and everything went dark as he approached his final seconds of life. Just as he prepared to close his eyes for the very last time, he took one final look at the river's bed, never before noticing how dry, wooden, and full of oxygen it was. The boy was shocked back to life as he realized that he was on all fours with his face to the floor of the art gallery. He panted for dear life, sucking in as much precious and abundant air as he could. His clothing remained bone dry. He fell back onto his rear and hung his head back, never so relieved to be able to breathe. After a moment of catching his breath, he raised his head, and mounted on the wall before his very eyes was Georges Seurat's *A Sunday Afternoon on the Island of La Grande Jatte.*

Chapter 6

The Time of Your Life

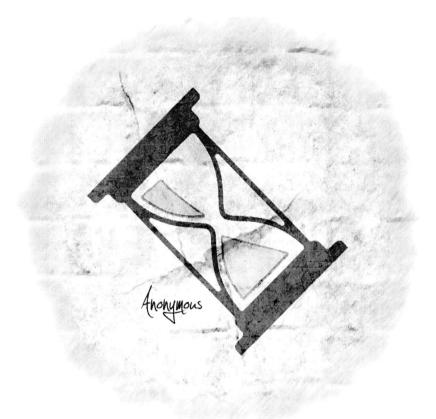

Anonymous

Lost time is never found again.
—BENJAMIN FRANKLIN

The boy clumsily rose to his feet, brushing himself off. He looked up to the painting mounted in front of him, squinting his eyes to sharpen his vision, afraid to get too close to it, remembering what happened the last time. His eyes carefully scanned the entire painting. His jaw dropped with disbelief as he recognized the two seated women and the woman fishing by the shore and the woman with a monkey on a leash. He could not believe his eyes as they settled, meeting those of a little girl dressed in white who appeared to be staring back at him. His heart skipped a beat as a bone-chilling sensation went through his body.

"It c-can't b-be," the boy fearfully stuttered.

"Oh contraire, my dear child!" a haunting voice said from behind.

The boy whipped his head over his shoulder as his body glaciated and went numb as the extravagantly dressed and ghastly man appeared before him.

"Hold on to that very thought," the man asserted, "for it is exactly what you were just thinking!"

The boy looked upon the ghastly man with disbelief, refusing to accept that all of this was not just a bad dream. The ghastly man rhythmically glided up to the boy who was too afraid to move, as if his legs were encased in cement. The boy looked up to the phantasmal creature, trembling as it glared down at him with its wicked grin.

"W-who are you?" the boy asked. "And what did you do to me? Why can't I remember my name?"

The ghastly man spewed a ghostly wail that shook the wall-mounted paintings down the entire hall. The boy took a step back, distancing himself from the looming presence of the ghastly man.

"Who am I?" he scoffed.

The ghastly man turned his back to the boy and slowly waded through the air away from him. Then he suddenly stopped and began to chuckle.

"Who am I, you ask?" the ghastly man continued.

"I am the whisper in your soul
The echo of silence, the reason why
Man painted on cave walls!
Quetzalcoatl to the Aztecs, Techne to the Greeks
A rose by any other name would smell as sweet![3]
I am the inspiration that guides your hand
The same hand that sculpted David[4]
And painted the Sistine Chapel ceiling![5]
I am the desire for something deeper
The source of creativity and innovation
I am passion, pain, and pleasure!
Visual music, freedom of expression!
The thread that weaves souls together!
The unspoken language of the heart
I am Palette, the spirit of art!"

The extravagantly dressed and ghastly man danced and swayed through the air as the flock of vibrantly colored parrots and birds of paradise and origami doves and cranes fluttered and flurried above, and the Japanese koi leapt in and out of the floor pond below. An awkward silence filled the hall. Only the melodic tune of a lone cricket's lullaby was heard as it chirped in applause of the art spirit's theatrical introduction. The boy, however, looked on with overwhelmed yet uninspired eyes. The left corner of his mouth unwillingly rose, forming into a slight smirk as the art spirit's over-the-top performance reminded him of someone else.

"What is it that you find to be so humorous?" Palette inquired.

"I-it's nothing!" the boy apologetically replied. "Anyway, you still have some explaining to do ... s-sir."

The art spirit released a heavy sigh as the flock of birds dispersed along with the glow of the koi's shimmering scales as they plunged into the depths of the floor.

"Very well, child," Palette said in a toned-down manner. "I shall give you the answers that you seek."

The boy looked upon the art spirit with expecting eyes, impatiently waiting to receive the answers he was so desperately seeking.

"Reach into your back pocket," Palette sternly said. "You will find an answer there."

The boy gave the art spirit a skeptical look, keeping his eyes on him as he cautiously reached into his back pocket and felt a stick-like object. The expression on his face changed from skeptical to curious as he removed the mysterious object and brought it within his sight. It was a paintbrush. Who would have thought? As the boy examined the paintbrush further, he came to the conclusion that it was no ordinary paintbrush.

"A paintbrush?" the boy questioned. "What's so special about this?"

The art spirit fiendishly chuckled.

"That, my dear child, is a gift," Palette said. "For as long as you possess that paintbrush, you will be granted the spectacular ability to enter into the worlds of paintings. But that is only the mere tip of the iceberg! Furthermore, you will also be granted the ability to bring whatever you create to life right before your very eyes!"

The boy was speechless. He wondered if such a tool could actually exist. It was no ordinary paintbrush. A dreamy look came to his face as his mind began to race, imagining all of the possibilities if what the art spirit said about the paintbrush was true. Suddenly, a waterfall of suspicion rushed down his face. As the boy marveled at the power that now lay in his hand, he realized that no downside had been presented.

"Hold up," the boy interjected. "Why would you give something like this to someone like me? What's the catch?"

The art spirit cracked a wicked grin. He began to chuckle uncontrollably. A bead of cold sweat ran down the side of the boy's face. He braced himself for the worst to happen as his curiosity had seemingly opened Pandora's box. He felt only regret for uttering the prying question from his lips. His anxiety began to destroy him from the inside out like a venomous viper's toxic bite as the art spirit's chuckle swelled into a hysterical cackle.

"'Tis answers you seek," Palette asserted, "then answers you shall find! Perhaps you should take a look at that photograph that you hold so dearly to your heart!"

The boy's eyes widened as he began feverishly rummaging through his pockets. He sighed in relief upon realizing that the photograph was still in his possession. As he scanned the photograph, he could not help but feel like something was not right. His attention fixated on an unfamiliar woman depicted in the picture.

"Who's this woman in my photograph?" he asked. "I don't remember her being in this picture."

"How ever could I possible know?" Palette said. "'Tis your photograph, after all. Is it not?"

A suspicious look came to the boy's face as he stared upon the untrustworthy demeanor of the art spirit.

"What's really going on?" the boy asked.

"You have known her for quite some time, if memory serves correctly," Palette claimed. "Perhaps this will jog your memory!"

The boy looked on with anticipation as the art spirit summoned the photograph replica portrait from before. The boy's heart dropped into the pit of his stomach. His eyes could not comprehend the meaning of what lay before him, and yet he had this sinking feeling that something dreadful was going on. His gaze traveled to and fro between the photograph and the portrait.

"W-what's going on?" the boy demanded. "Why is the woman faded away in the portrait but not in the photograph? It wasn't like that before!"

"'Tis for the same reason you cannot remember your own name, my dear child," Palette snickered.

The boy went into a panic as he suddenly became short of breath. It was uncertain as to whether or not he fully understood the gravity of the situation or if his mind was refusing to accept what he already knew in his heart.

"W-what do y-you mean?" the boy asked.

"You have been lost for quite some time now," Palette solemnly said. "That is why you must find what you have been so desperately searching for, for so long. The reason you cannot remember the woman in the photograph is because her image has been erased from your memory, so to speak. This portrait you see before you contains all of the memories of your past—everything you knew, everyone you loved, everything that defined who you were, your identity. As time goes on, the portrait will continue to gradually fade, and with it, your oh-so-precious memories of who you once were—that is, unless you can solve the riddle of your heart and unbind the spell. Till then, your fate belongs in the hands of time."

The boy remained deathly silent, at a complete loss for words as the art spirit's body began fading away.

"I do encourage you to tour the gallery," Palette firmly suggested. "Perhaps you will find some inspiration within the art. But be fore-warned; you will find the gallery to be quite different from what you remember. If ever you find yourself to be lost, seek direction from the art. And remember:

> "What you seek is within the heart—
> And there you will find the Lost Art."

The art spirit vanished without leaving behind a single trace of his existence. Only a cold, dark, and empty hallway remained. The boy folded down to his knees, staring off into the blackness. There was only darkness as far as his eyes could see, with no assurance of a light at the end of the tunnel. He was looking into the pit of despair. The boy embraced himself in his arms to weather the cold loneliness of the hallway as tears began to form in his eyes.

Chapter 7
Shooting for the Stars

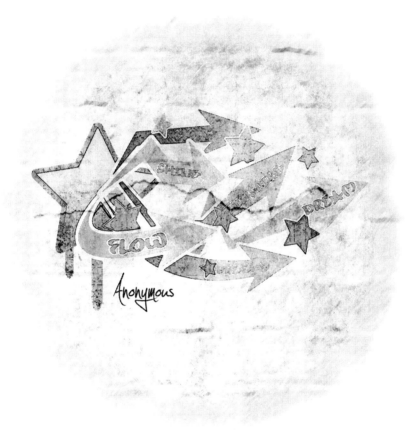

Anonymous

Gently drifting among the stars,
Waves of wind maneuver my kite.
Flashing lights and boisterous cars
Bustling bellow the starry night.
I will go where the wind takes me.

* * * ??:?? * * *

The boy securely fastened his arms around his legs, tightly pulling his knees to his chest. His low-hanging chin gently rested on his knees as tears flowed down his face like two neighboring streams. Several minutes passed as he wallowed in his self-pity. He took another look at the photograph in his pocket and began to reminisce. As his eyes focused on the woman whom he could no longer remember, he began to imagine the fate of his remaining memories. He stood and wiped his eyes on his sleeve as his sniffling began to ease. Suddenly, the walls began to groan, and the floor began to rumble. The boy lost his footing and was slung into the wall as the world around him began violently shaking.

Now what? the boy thought.

The tremor lasted for only a minute or so as the boy unstably walked alongside the wall, barely able to keep his balance. The hall was so dark that he could only see a few feet in front of him. He cautiously made his way down the hall with uncertain steps, slowly inching forward, putting one foot in front of the other, step by step by step.

"I'd watch where ya goin', kiddo," an unknown voice warned. "The next step's a real doozy!"

The startled boy pushed back from the wall in alarm. He looked around, trying to find the source of the unknown voice.

"Pssst … right in front of ya, kiddo!" the unknown voice whispered.

The boy looked to the wall that he was previously clinging to, only to discover a mounted lithograph printing. The lithograph printing depicted a room full of crazy staircases that ran in all directions. He carefully examined it to learn that the lithograph printing was called *Relativity* by M. C. Escher.

"H-hello?" the boy timidly asked.

"Hiya!" the lithograph printing enthusiastically answered. "My name is Relativity, but my friends call me Crazy Stairs. You look like a first timer here. It's my job to make sure you understand how things work around here!"

"So you know what that earthquake was about?" the boy asked.

The lithograph printing laughed. The boy looked at it, not understanding the humor in his question.

"That was no earthquake, kiddo," Crazy Stairs asserted. "The architectural structure of this place likes to rotate from time to time, and each time the place rotates, the layout of the hallways changes with it, so the maze is always changin'."

"Maze?"

"Yep! You're standin' right on top of one big combination puzzle labyrinth. Well, technically we're on the bottom of it now after that last rotation, but hey, it's all relative anyway!"

The boy looked upon the lithograph printing with a dazed expression. He could not comprehend a word of anything the lithograph printing was saying.

"Lemme break it down to ya another way," Crazy Stairs explained. "Think of this place as a giant Rubik's Cube. Things can be a little topsy-turvy here since normal laws of gravity don't apply. Upside down, right side up, or even sideways, it doesn't matter! A floor is a floor. It's all relative! You were about to learn that the hard way had you taken one more step!"

The boy was intrigued by the lithograph printing's explanation, though he did not completely understand. He turned his attention down the hall in the direction that he had been walking. As he looked out into the distance, all he could see was an infinite expanse of darkness. He tilted his head downward and noticed that the floor had been cut off like a cliff. Confused, he carefully leaned forward to peer down over the edge. The boy was astonished to discover that the cliff face was another hallway leading vertically downward.

"You expect me to just walk down this hall?" the boy asked. "I'd be a goner for sure."

"Remember, everything is relative here!" Crazy Stairs asserted. "A floor is a floor, so just take a step of faith!"

The boy took a gulp as he turned to the lithograph printing one last time. He gradually inched the toes of his shoes to the edge of the floor as he looked down the face of the vertical hallway. He closed his eyes and began slowly counting in his head.

"Three, two, one!" the boy shouted as he stepped over the edge.

Seconds later, nothing happened. His eyes stayed closed for a moment and then slowly creaked open. He found that he was standing right side up on the edge of the vertically hanging hallway, yet he was not falling. Everything was relative, after all. Who would have thought? The boy began roaming the maze of hallways, with no sense of direction. As he traveled the unfamiliar halls, he noticed that several new paintings had been added to the gallery. His eyes wondered left and right until finally he came across an oddly familiar painting. It was Vincent van Gogh's *The Starry Night,* yet there was something different about it. There were no stars in the sky. As the boy peered into the deep and dark sky of the painting, he remembered the words of the art spirit. He leaned in closer to examine the painting, reaching his hand out to touch it. Just as the tips of his fingers grazed its surface, it began to ripple like water. The boy quickly retracted his hand in shock, forgetting that this was one of his new abilities. He reached into his back pocket to remove the bizarre paintbrush and studied it closely. He returned his attention to the painting as the paintbrush began glowing with a mystical aura.

"Within the heart, huh?" the boy murmured to himself. "Well, here it goes!"

The boy closed his eyes and dove head first into *The Starry Night.* Moments later, a strange feeling engulfed his body. A brief sensation of falling gripped him for just an instant and then dissipated just as quickly. He felt his stomach abandon his body as everything else became weightless. He was blinded and deafened by the strong pressure of whipping wind in his face, which forced his eyes shut and jamming his ears. The temperature of his skin began to drop as the dynamic air around him cooled. As the boy pried open his eyes, the ground approached him from thousands of feet below. He opened his mouth to scream in terror as the wind immediately silenced him, smothering his breath as if setting a television to mute. His heart stopped, and his limbs thrashed wildly through the air as he realized that he was free falling right out of the deep and dark sky of *The Starry Night*. No place for someone who did not have wings. Panic set in as the boy's mind went blank. His back turned to the ground as his thrashing caused him to tumble midair. As he looked up into the sky above him, he saw the bizarre paintbrush free falling just within his reach. The boy reached for the paintbrush and was struck with inspiration just as it came into his grasp. Without thinking, he madly motioned his arm to paint four, broad brush strokes with connecting corners, forming a large diamond. He began filling the interior of the diamond shape's outline and closed his eyes upon its completion.

"I hope this works!" the boy hollered.

Suddenly, his stomach returned to his body. His weight was restored as his limbs became heavy once again. The whipping wind calmed to a gentle breeze as the sensation of falling was replaced by the comfort of a solid platform underneath his feet. The boy opened his eyes to discover that he was no longer falling but rather gently drifting through the sky, mounted on a vibrantly colored kite made of paint. The boy began laughing with merriment as he surfed on the wind, with the French village of Saint-Rémy below.

"That actually worked!" the boy said with a sigh of relief.

The boy wiped the cold sweat from his brow as he leisurely lay back on the kite. He closed his eyes to catch a moment of relaxation before figuring out his next move.

"Who dares to enter my domain?" an omnipotent voice bellowed.

The boy joltingly propped up, caught off guard by the powerful voice. As he looked around, he appeared to be alone; as all he could see was broad, open sky.

"I-I don't remember my name," the boy meekly responded. "I'm looking for something and hoped I'd find it here."

"I see," the omnipotent voice bellowed. "I too know what it feels like to have lost something. My sky was once filled with magnificent stars that inspired all of those who gazed upon them. However, the stars have gone, and with them, the wonder of the night sky."

A compassionate expression came to the boy's face as he

sympathized with the omnipotent voice of the sky. He thought back on how *The Starry Night* painting captured his own imagination during his tour with the tall, slender man. After a moment of silence, he looked to the bizarre paintbrush in his hand as it once again began glowing with a mystical aura. He tightly clenched the brush and looked up into the deep and dark sky.

"Maybe I can help," the boy offered. "I'm no van Gogh, but I can give it my best shot."

Several seconds went by without a response. The boy began to lower his head in defeat, foolishly thinking that he was talented enough to actually restore such a magnificent painting. He motioned to return the paintbrush to his back pocket.

"So be it," the omnipotent voice bellowed. "I shall trust your abilities, young artist, for I have already seen what you are capable of. In return, I shall help you find what you are looking for."

The boy's eyes lit up with excitement. It was not everyday that *The Starry Night* asked you to repaint its stars, after all. He pulled the bizarre paintbrush back out, invigorated by the omnipotent voice's reassuring words of faith. He took a deep breath and closed his eyes. He searched through his imagination in order to find a source of inspiration that would guide his brush strokes. Once again, the little girl's sweet words came to mind:

> *Imagine a sky filled with stars—*
> *Like freeing fireflies from jars.*

He began to imagine himself in a wide-open field with the little girl dressed in white as they frolicked through the park collecting fireflies in jars, preparing to release them into the night sky. As the boy painted this image in his mind, he remembered the promise he made to her.

"I made a promise to a friend that I'd show her what a starlit night looks like," the boy proclaimed. "I will keep my promise!"

The boy stood as if he were riding his skateboard and began swiftly drifting and gliding across the deep and dark sea in the sky. He used the paintbrush to quickly create a pair of vibrantly colored goggles to protect his eyes from the whipping wind. He securely fastened them over his determination-filled eyes as a sly grin came to his face. As he became comfortable with maneuvering the kite, he began painting several tiny five-pointed shapes.

"I guess this is where the phrase 'shoot for the stars' comes from!" the boy shouted.

The boy launched a handful of tiny, five-pointed stars into the air. He watched with expectancy as the glittering shards began to disperse in the sky like fireflies. Suddenly, several large booms sounded as the tiny five-pointed stars began bursting into bright, burning orbs of light. The radiant glows of the stars reflected off of the boy's goggles, concealing his awestruck eyes. A splendid smile came to his face as he continued hurling handfuls of stars, plastering the night sky through a celestial show of pyrotechnics. The popping and crackling of bursting orbs of light filled the air as the deep and dark sky magically ignited like the grand finale of a fireworks display on the Fourth of July. The boy raised his goggles from over his eyes as his work was completed. He took a seat on the kite with his legs dangling over the edge, gracefully surfing on waves of wind now among a sea of stars.

"You have restored the wonder to my sky," the omnipotent voice bellowed. "For this, I am eternally grateful."

"Don't sweat it!" the boy said with a smile. "It was fun. I'm just glad I could help. And thanks for believing in me."

"Unfortunately, what you are looking for is not here," the omnipotent voice bellowed, "but as promised, I shall guide you to your next destination. Remember this:

> "A helping hand to you I lend—
> Just follow the flow of the wind."

A puzzled look came to the boy's face as he attempted to decipher the clue. He crossed his arms and furrowed his brow and began meditating as he looked up into the deep and dark sky.

"Just follow the flow?" the boy asked. "That's your profound advice?"

"Fear not, young artist," the omnipotent voice bellowed. "The answer shall come to you in due time."

Before the boy could ask any further questions, he clumsily crashed into the gallery hallway wall across from *The Starry Night* painting.

Chapter 8
Gone with the Wind

Anonymous

The stiffest tree is more easily
cracked, while the bamboo or willow
survives by bending with the wind.
—BRUCE LEE

The boy stumbled to his feet, dizzy headed, as the room around him spun. The world around him returned to a standstill, and his kite merged into the wall like a piece of graffiti art. He kneeled down to look at the painting of the kite closely, scratching it with his finger to see if it was wet.

"And to think, I was the one who didn't want to tag anything in here," the boy said while shaking his head. "I hope I don't get in trouble for this."

Suddenly, the hall began violently shaking as the gallery's next rotation commenced. The boy was thrown off balance with his back against the wall, clinging on for dear life. The bizarre paintbrush in his tightly clutched hand began to glow as he pressed his body against the wall with all his might. He strained to flatten himself as much as possible as his body unexpectedly began merging into the wall. Much to his surprise, he was no longer affected by the shaking of the room, and as his portrait body began to move in unison with the quaking halls. Moments later, the walls ceased their groaning, and the floors calmed their rumbling; the hall became still once again. The boy peeled himself off of the wall, and his body returned to its normal state. He began frantically patting himself down, as if checking to make sure that everything was still there.

"So I can even turn myself into a painting?" the boy said to himself. "That spirit guy definitely left that part out."

As he continued to pat himself down, he felt a slight breeze caress his face. The boy raised his head to see *The Starry Night* painting hanging directly in front of him. He reached out toward the painting, blocking the gentle breeze with his hand as a cunning smile came to his face.

"Follow the flow of the wind!" the boy joyfully said to himself.

The boy stepped back from the painting, ready to follow the direction of the wind. He walked back a few feet only to realize that the wind stream was too weak for him to detect over an extended distance. Stumped, he sat down on the floor with crisscrossed legs, folded arms, and a perplexed face. His adventure within *The Starry Night* played back in his head as he attempted to uncover the hidden key to his current puzzle. His imagination started to run wild, losing track of the issue at hand as he began to reflect on the peacefulness of floating on the wind like a weightless butterfly in the breeze.

"That's it!" the boy exalted.

The boy eagerly began stroking the outline of two heart shapes that connected at the corners with the bizarre paintbrush. As he filled in the lines, the two heart-shaped flaps started to flutter. The boy stepped back as a vibrantly colored butterfly took off from the tip of the paintbrush. The butterfly aimlessly frolicked through the air as the boy carefully used his hands to guide its path toward the painting. As the butterfly finally made its way in front of the painting, it continued fluttering on its own accord, unshaken by the breeze.

It must be too heavy, the boy thought.

As the boy pondered the issue, he suddenly heard a faint, crinkling noise. He turned his attention down the hall and noticed a stray sheet of paper curiously coasting along the floor.

What's this doing here? the boy wondered.

The blank sheet of paper was as colorless and uninspired as the boy's white, hooded sweatshirt. He held the blank sheet of paper in his hand as he began to think of all of the ways in which he could use his newfound abilities.

"All right then," the boy said to himself. "Time to think outside the box."

Moments later, it finally came to him. The boy began creasing and folding the sheet of paper in a series of steps, creating an origami butterfly. As the completed paper insect lay lifelessly in his hands, he pulled out the paintbrush.

"Paper is lighter than paint," the boy confidently said to himself. "This should work."

As the boy lightly dabbed a droplet of paint onto the origami butterfly's wing, it miraculously sprung to life. Amazed at his own feat, he carefully guided it back toward the painting, where it immediately caught the airstream and began gently drifting down the hall in the wind's current. The boy casually strolled after the paper insect down the halls, wondering where it would finally come to a stop. As the boy made his way down the hall, he heard faint, painful cries emitting from a dark, abstract painting depicting suffering people and animals surrounded by buildings wreaked with violence and destruction. The suffering people moaned and groaned in agony, calling out to the boy as he passed by. The boy read the dark, abstract painting to be *Guernica* by Pablo Picasso. He quickly turned away from the unsettling cries of the suffering painting.

He continued down a haunted hall of African art as mask sculptures antagonized and tormented him with their ghostly wails of tribal chants. The strange-looking African masks frightened him as their dark, hollowed eyes peered into his soul. He could not shake the feeling that the hall was hexed as he timidly continued to walk with a shaken spirit. The boy hastily made his way around the corner to discover that the butterfly had settled in front of a mounted painting on another dead-ended wall. The boy eagerly sprinted toward the end of the hall, ready to dive into whatever the painting might be. As he approached, his feet abruptly came to a stop. An eerie sensation overcame his body as he realized the identity of the painting that held an ominous, blood-orange sky. An unshakable feeling of fear encased him as his knees started to buckle and shiver.

W-where did the guy in the painting go? the boy thought.

He stood in front of the paining for several minutes, too afraid to move forward. He gently caged the delicate butterfly in his hands and walked back down the hall, away from the unsettling painting. As he reached the hallway intersection, he released the butterfly from his hands, hoping that it mistakenly detoured down the wrong path. Upon release, the butterfly immediately fluttered down the same dead-end hallway and settled in front of the unsettling painting. A grim expression came to the boy's face as he grudgingly made his way toward the painting. He took a deep breath and slowly crawled into *The Scream*.

Chapter 9
Silence Is Golden

Shy of the self within my dreams
The madness grows within my mind.
Devoured in this world of screams
Are silent truths I hope to find.
My thoughts are my worst enemy.

The sky erupted like a violent volcano, staining the air with a blistering, blood-orange hue. It loomed over the ground below like a floating pool of molten lava. All living creatures took refuge under the punishing sky for fear that at any moment it would rain down upon them with fire and brimstone as it once did in the ancient cities of Sodom and Gomorrah. The world was quiet and empty, and the road lay void of any cars or pedestrians, very different from the lively hustle and bustle of the Arts District. The deafening silence pierced through the boy's eardrums like screeching nails clawing at a chalkboard. He could sense immediately that there was something foul in the air of this distortedly colored world. He cautiously crossed the isolated and deserted, winding hill road and approached an overlook. A dark, lifeless city lay dormant in the distance next to a large body of water. There was neither a single light that visibly emitted from the city nor a single boat's sail on the water's dark, rolling waves. A spine-chilling sensation coursed through the boy's bones as he looked into the ominous sky.

"Gowayyy!" a shrieking voice cried.

The boy nearly jumped out of his skin. He swiftly swiveled his head, scanning his surroundings for the sound's source. His nerves began to settle as he started to believe that it was just his imagination.

"*Gowayyy!*" the shrieking voice cried again.

The startled boy jumped yet again in response to the squawking cry. He was now convinced that he was not alone after all. His paranoia heightened as he sensed the presence of another living creature, though he could not determine its identity or whereabouts.

"*Gowayyy!*" the shrieking voice screamed.

As the boy sharply swung his head over his shoulder, he discovered a gray bird casually perched on the rail of the overlook. Its dull, smoky-gray feathers were as colorless and uninspired as the gray clouds that cloaked the Arts District, like the soot from a dusty chimney. It stared at the boy with its black, beady eyes, unblinking, as if it were probing through his very thoughts to reveal his deepest and darkest fears.

"It's just a bird," the boy said with a sigh of relief.

The gray bird continued to stare at the boy with its black, beady, and unblinking eyes, cocking its head from side to side in a rather inquisitive manner. The boy began to feel insecure as the gray bird continued to violate his privacy with its penetrating gaze. He slowly made his way down the road as to figure out his next move, relieving himself of the creepy, gray bird's sight.

"Gowayyy!" the grey bird shrieked from a distance. "Gowayyy!"

The boy shuttered, afraid to look back as the gray bird continued to torment him with its disturbing cry. As the boy made his way down the road, he once again got the feeling he was not alone. Suddenly, he heard a silent whisper echo from behind. He quickly jerked his body around to identify the mysterious presence, only to find no one there. He closed his eyes and slowly counted to three, heavily concentrating on his breathing. As his panting returned to a calmer pace, he turned back around and continued down the winding hill road.

There's nothing to be afraid of, the boy thought to himself. *I'm the only one here. It's all in my head.*

As the boy calmly continued down the road, he looked up to yet again realize that he was not alone. Several gray birds were perched on the power lines overlooking the road, all with black, beady, and unblinking eyes staring at him.

"Gowayyy!" the gray birds shrieked. "Gowayyy!"

The boy turned his attention back down the road, attempting to ignore the shrieking and squawking of the menacing gray birds. His hands began shaking as more and more of the gray birds began landing on street signs and trees, all with black, beady, and unblinking eyes staring at him.

"Gowayyy!" the gray birds shrieked. "Gowayyy! Go away!"

The boy's eyes widened, and his heart stopped.

D-did that bird just speak? the boy thought. *N-no it couldn't have. It's just in my head.*

As the gray birds continued shrieking and squawking, flocking around the boy by the dozens, his calm walk turned into a hurried jog and then a desperate, all-out dash. His heart pounded, and his breaths shortened as droplets of cold sweat flung from his brow. He could hear the frenzied flapping of wings and antagonizing cries of the birds closing in on him from behind, suffocating him with their noise. Just as the boy motioned to turn his head back at the swarm of preying birds, he was startled as one swooped into his face. He reflexively swiped at the aggressive, gray bird with the bizarre paintbrush, sending a slicing wave of paint through its feathery body. His face drowned in terror as the gray bird exploded into a thick, black substance, like a water balloon filled with sludge. The boy stood frozen as the black ink rained down on him, staining his clothing and splashing on his hands and face. A strange sensation overcame his body as the black ink made contact with his exposed skin. His blood ran cold, and his skin went numb. His heart pounded, and his breath thinned. His eyes widened, and his pupils dilated. His palms sweated, and his hands trembled. His ears rang as the sensation of vertigo began setting in, causing his vision to blur and his balance to waver. The paintbrush slipped from the grasp of his fingers and dropped to the ground. He raised his ink-spattered hand to his face, closely examining it as it trembled.

W-what is t-this f-f-feeling? the boy thought.

Fear. The boy was consumed with fear. This fear, however, was no ordinary fear. This fear seeped into the depths of his soul, staining it with its thick, black ink. It seeped into the darkest corners of his mind and fed off of his imagination. It was neither explicable nor rational. It simply was. The boy was consumed with fear in its purest and most genuine form. Fear for fear's sake. No ordinary fear indeed.

"EMBRACE THE FEAR!" a screaming voice echoed through the boy's mind. "LET IT CONSUME YOU!"

The boy fell to his knees in a state of complete hysteria as saliva began trickling down the corner of his gaping mouth.

"AREN'T YOU TIRED OF BEING A BURDEN TO THE ONES YOU LOVE?"

"YOU WORTHLESS CHILD!"

"YOU DON'T EVEN REMEMBER WHO YOU ARE!"

"YOU'RE ALL ALONE!"

"FEAR IS THE ONLY FRIEND YOU HAVE IN THIS WORLD!"

"LET IT DEVOUR YOU!"

The boy raised his trembling, ink-spattered hands to cover his ears, depleting his last reserve of energy. His attempt to silence the world around him failed as the agonizing screams resonated in his head. He closed his eyes as tears began to trickle down his face, and he collapsed into a fetal position with his hands over his ears. He tried to imagine being in a happier place, only for his positive thoughts to be devoured by fear. His memories of the little girl dressed in white and painting the wonderful, starlit sky became blotted with black ink, erasing them from his memory. Everything became lost within this dark world of screams.

"Don't give up," a gentle voice called to the boy. "Your masterpiece is not yet complete. You have more painting to do."

Suddenly, the boy's mind stopped racing. He mustered the strength to rise to a knee. His breathing calmed as he stood amidst the chaos of the world around him. He confidently removed his hands from over his ears. The screaming had stopped. A calm overcame his body, as if a hurricane's gale force winds had abruptly disbanded without warning. His inner storm had vanished. The boy opened his eyes to realize that he was back in the gallery hall. A tender smile came to his face.

I guess the world isn't so loud after all, the boy thought to himself.

He looked up to *The Scream* painting on the wall in front of him and noticed that it had been restored with the original image of the agonized man. He looked the agonized man in the face and smiled.

"So it was all just in my head after all," the boy said with a snicker. "Who would've thought?"

Chapter 10
Straight as an Arrow

Efforts and courage are not enough
without purpose and direction.
-JOHN F. KENNEDY

The boy hastily reached into the pocket of his hooded sweatshirt and pulled out the photograph. The unfamiliar woman in the photograph was now holding a newborn baby in her arms that he could not identify. He clenched his fist and returned the photograph to his pocket, turning his attention back to *The Scream*.

"Hey!" the boy shouted.

There was no response. A large vein in the boy's forehead began to twitch and throb, impatiently waiting for a response from the painting. His foot vigorously tapped against the wooden floor, growing more impatient.

"*Answer me!*" the boy screamed.

"What?" the agonized man responded. "Did you say something?"

"Can you help me?" the boy impatiently asked. "I could really use some directions."

Several seconds passed as neither the boy nor the agonized man spoke. Again, the agonized man ignored the boy. The boy's patience ran thin.

"Hey!" the boy screamed. "Are you even listening to me?"

"What?" the agonized man responded. "Do you need something?"

The boy looked at the agonized man with furious eyes. He began to wonder if the agonized man was simply playing some sort of game with him—a game he did not have time to play. He then noticed that the agonized man was covering his ears. He suddenly realized that the agonized man was not ignoring him but simply could not hear him.

"I need directions!" the boy yelled. "I don't have a lot of time left!"

"What?" the agonized man screamed.

"I said I need directions!" the boy screamed.

"You need directions?" the agonized man screamed. "Why didn't you just say so in the first place?"

The boy's face straightened, appalled at the agonized man's comment.

"Remember this sequence!" the agonized man screamed. "Up, right, right, down, left, up, left, down, up!"

The boy looked upon the painting with a puzzled face. Suddenly, his face lit up.

"Up, right, right," the boy murmured. "This must be the path through the hallways!"

As the boy turned away from the painting and down the hall, he realized that the hallways had rotated since he was last in them. There was no hall to the right or left for him to turn down.

"I don't understand!" the boy screamed. "The hallways have changed, and there's no way for me to turn right!"

"Just go down this hall and keep going straight as an arrow," the agonized man screamed. "You can't miss it!"

The boy was still unsure of the agonized man's directions. He hesitantly turned away from the painting to make his way down the hall.

"One more thing!" the agonized man screamed. Remember this:

"Paint the arrows as they appear—
And the passage will be made clear."

The boy's confusion only deepened. With no other options, he made his way down the solitary, dead-end hall. As he approached the end of the hall, he noticed nine canvases mounted on the wall, neatly aligned in three rows and three columns. He looked upon them curiously as he realized that all nine of the canvases were blank.

"Hiya, kiddo!" a familiar voice called from the sidewall. "Fancy runnin' into you again. What are the odds?"

"It's you," the boy said. "Umm … who are you again?"

"Don't tell me you already forgot your best bud, Crazy Stairs!" the lithograph printing said. "Ya breakin' my heart, kiddo!"

The boy approached the lithograph printing.

"Oh yeah, that's right!" the boy said. "Sorry, my memory isn't what it used to be."

"I hear ya, kiddo!" Crazy Stairs said. "Happens to the best of us!"

The boy turned his attention back to the nine blank canvases on the wall.

"So what's the deal with these?" the boy asked.

"I'm glad ya asked!" Crazy Stairs said. "What you're lookin' at right now is the Canvas Control System. You can use these canvases here to manually control the maze's rotations! And to think, you happened to stumble upon it and me at the same time. What are the odds? You're one lucky kid, kiddo! Well, relatively speaking, with all things considered, of course."

"So you know how to operate this thing?" the boy asked.

"Of course!" Crazy Stairs responded. "After all, it's my job to show ya how things work in this place, remember?"

The boy released a sigh of relief as a smile came to his face. Things were finally looking his way.

"Only problem is that ya need to know where ya wanna go in order to make it work," Crazy Stairs asserted. "Do you by any chance have any directions for where ya wanna go?"

The boy folded his arms and lowered his head. He raked through his muddled mind of tattered memories, trying to find the missing piece to the puzzle.

"So there are nine canvases," the boy whispered to himself.

The boy began pacing back and forth, deeply lost in thought as he tried to decipher his clues thus far.

"Up, right, right, down, left, up, left, down, up," the boy whispered. "That's it! The screaming guy gave me nine directions!"

"Whoa, look at you!" Crazy Stairs shouted. "Nice detective skills, kiddo!"

"But what am I supposed to do with these directions?" the boy asked.

"And this is where your favorite, handy-dandy labyrinth manual comes in!" Crazy Stairs said. "The key to activatin' the system is right there in ya back pocket!"

A mystified expression came to the boy's face as he reached into his back pocket. He pulled out the bizarre paintbrush and closely studied it.

"You mean this?" the boy asked. "And how exactly do I use this to make the hallways move?"

"Use your head, kiddo!" Crazy Stairs responded. "You already know the answer!"

The boy turned back to the nine canvases mounted on the wall. He shifted his attention back and forth from the paintbrush and the nine canvases, looking for the missing link.

Paint the arrows as they appear—
And the passage will be made clear.

Up, right, right, down, left, up, left, down, up," the boy thought. ↑, →, →, ↓, ←, ↑, ←, ↓, ↑

A sly grin came to the boy's face as the bizarre paintbrush started to glow. He had finally figured it out.

"Well, here goes nothing!" the boy shouted.

The boy gripped the paintbrush and spiritedly swiped it skyward onto the top left canvas, topping the vertical stroke with an upward arc. A few seconds went by as nothing happened. The boy slowly lowered his arm, confused by the anticlimactic response of the hallways. Seconds later, the walls began to groan, and the floors began to rumble as the gallery's rotation went under way. The boy jumped with elation as he continued painting the arrows.

"Right! Right! Down! Left!" the boy chanted in unison with his strokes.

As the boy approached the last few inputs, the wall holding the lithograph printing began to pull away. He turned his attention to the lithograph printing as it and the wall departed.

"It's been real, kiddo!" Crazy Stairs shouted. "Looks like this is where we go our separate ways! Good luck on the rest of your journey, and I hope ya find what you're lookin' for!"

The boy gave the lithograph printing a gracious smile and waved it off as it pulled further and further away. He turned his attention back to the nine canvases, ready to input the final arrow.

"One last thing!" Crazy Stairs warned. "The code you just input will return the gallery's hallways back to their original layout of parallel rows and will lead you to the gallery's secret hall. The rotation won't last for long, so don't dilly-dally. It's a long hallway, kiddo!"

"Now he tells me," the boy said under his breath. "Better get ready to move then."

As the final rotation of his nine-arrow code approached a standstill, the boy stood ready atop a vibrantly colored skateboard with a large sail attached. The final countdown commenced.

"Straight as an arrow, huh?" the boy smirked to himself.

"Three …"

The boy lowered his vibrantly colored goggles over his eyes.

"Two …"

He opened the vibrantly colored sail of the skateboard.

"One …"

He rapidly began swirling and whirling the paintbrush in the air behind him.

"Let's go!" the boy shouted.

The boy furiously kicked the floor, advancing the skateboard as a vibrantly colored whirlwind caught the sail, whipping him forward at breakneck speed. The grinding growl of skateboard wheels and the sound of wind whipping through the sail filled the air as the boy parasailed down the hall, swiftly drifting and gliding on the wooden sea. His cheeks and nostrils filled with air as his immense speed transformed the gallery hall into a wind tunnel, moving through the stretch like a torpedo. As he made his way down the hall, the walls began to groan, and the floor began to rumble. The boy turned his head over his shoulder to see the hallways had begun to rotate from behind. He turned his attention forward as a concentrated look came to his face. There was no more looking back. His eyes ignited, burning with determination as he focused his attention to the end of the hall that was still out of his sight. As he came down to the final home stretch, he could feel the hall disappearing behind him, quickly creeping on him like a cheetah stalking its prey. The boy's heart started pounding as his breath began to thin. The hairs on his skin stood on end, and his palms turned sweaty. His blood ran cold, and his bones began to quiver. Was it fear that had consumed the boy once again? No. There was something different in the boy's eyes. The flames of his spirit would not be extinguished, blazing and burning with an unstoppable desire to succeed. He would not fail. The overbearing walls continued to close in on him, getting closer and closer. He kept his gaze on the end of the long, dark hallway, convinced that there was a light of hope at the end of the tunnel. Through the dark haze, a mounted painting finally appeared within the boy's vision. His eyes lit up with promise. As he tried to make out the identity of the painting, a closing wall clipped his back wheels, sending him hurling off of the skateboard. Time came to a standstill as the boy's body floated through the air. He had fallen short of the mark. This was the end of the road for his journey, after he had come so far. Who would have thought that it would end like this? As time came back into play, the boy was flung forward, right into the mystery painting like a dart. It was a bull's eye after all. Who would have thought?

Chapter 11
Just Keep Smiling

Anonymous

A troublesome look stains her face
Unlike her ordinary style.
World renowned for her unmatched grace.
So why then does she not smile?
She is truly a masterpiece.

The fresh scent of crisp, mountainous air filled the boy's lungs as he took in a deep breath through his nostrils. He felt the cool touch of damp earth on his skin as he placed his hand into the ground's rich, dark soil. The air was cool and moist, saturated with morning dew. A hush came over the world, highlighting the natural sounds of running water and the cheerful chirping of birds. The boy stood to take in the beautiful scenery as the landscape around him transformed into a musical theater, and the flora and fauna danced to the serene sounds of Mother Nature's soothing symphony. In the distance lay a vast countryside of valleys and rivers that retreated into an icy range of majestic mountains painted on the horizon. It was a natural sanctuary. If it were not for the presence of the solitary bridge and the system of twisting dirt paths, there would not be a single trace of artificial creation by human hands. As he looked off into the distance, he saw the figure of a seated person, pasted against the breathtaking backdrop. The boy gazed in awe, enthralled at the magnificence of the imagery as he approached the seated person.

"Hello there," the woman properly said. "'Tis a pleasure to make your acquaintance. How do you do?"

She was the most elegant woman the boy had ever laid his eyes upon. She sat in a reserved, upright position with a perfectly proper posture. Her tender hands lay gently folded on the armrest of her chair, distancing herself from the boy as he approached. The light reflected on her delicate skin, causing it to glow with a radiant, golden hue. Her long, brunette hair neatly flowed down her shoulders like a waterfall, pouring into the dark veils of her garment. She was rather elegant indeed.

"H-hi," the boy bashfully responded. "I was wondering if you could help me."

The elegant woman looked at the boy with disdainful eyes. She turned her head to the side, sticking her nose in the air.

"Humph!" the elegant woman scoffed. "'Tis quite rude to ask one for a favor before proper introductions are made."

An embarrassed expression came to the boy's face. He bowed his head with a flushed face.

"S-sorry!" the boy apologized. "But I unfortunately can't remember my name."

The elegant woman looked at the boy sideways, sharply turning her vision downward in a condescending manner.

"'Tis rather unfortunate, indeed," the woman replied. "At any rate, I shall properly introduce myself. My name is Lisa Giocondo, wife of Francesco del Giocondo. 'Tis a pleasure to make your acquaintance."

The boy raised his head to meet the eyes of the elegant woman. He noticed that she had a rather distraught look on her face. The corners of her lips turned downward ever so slightly, creating a subtle frown on her face. The boy studied her face intently, trying to remember where he had seen the elegant woman before, yet his memory yielded nothing.

"Excuse me?" the boy asked with concern. "Is there something bothering you? You look sad."

The woman looked at the boy with astonishment, surprised at the boldness of his question.

"Humph!" Lisa scoffed. "'Tis quite rude to …"

The woman abruptly paused in midsentence. A troublesome look came to her face.

This young boy actually cares, Lisa thought to herself.

She softly sighed, and her stern expression slowly sank into one of sorrow. Her tender, folded hands anxiously fidgeted as she bit her bottom lip, looking for the words to say to the young boy that stood before her.

"Perhaps there is something that is troubling me," Lisa grieved. "I was not always a painting. Long ago, I lived as a person, as the woman in my portrait. I was the wife of a very wealthy silk merchant who lived in Florence in the sixteenth century.[6] This was at the same time that I met the great Renaissance artist, Leonardo de Vinci, the very man who painted my portrait."

The boy looked on intently as the elegant woman continued to tell her story.

"Sir da Vinci was a true Renaissance man. So filled with imagination and a spirit for invention. He was truly a man before his time. I could sense that there was something special about him from the moment I first laid eyes on him. I had always thought myself to be an ordinary woman, no different than the next. I tried my very best to be a loving mother and supportive wife to my husband, nothing more, nothing less. I never imagined that there would be anything special about me. That is, until I met Sir da Vinci. He was fascinated with me. He saw something within me that I could not see myself. He made me feel important. He made me feel that I was of some use. He made me feel … special. Since then, his soul has lived on within my painting, as I have become the best known, the most visited, the most written about, the most sung about, and the most parodied work of art in the world."

"Wow!" the boy gasped with excitement. "It must be really cool to be that popular. I mean, to be able to go anywhere, and everybody knows your name. For everybody to acknowledge you …"

The boy's expression changed. His chin lowered, and his gaze shifted to the ground. He began to scavenge through the remains of his memories, unable to recall a single person who would care whether or not he ever reclaimed his identity from the art spirit. The elegant woman looked at the sorrowful boy with concern in her eyes.

"If you are so loved by everyone," the boy asked, "then why are you so unhappy?"

The elegant woman was once again taken aback by the boy's question. Silence slowly crept its way into the conversation, filling the void with the serene sounds of nature. She gracefully raised her hand to her radiantly glowing face and gently wiped a tear from her eye.

"Because Sir da Vinci was the only person that could make me smile," Lisa sorrowfully said.

The boy looked at the elegant woman with grief as she began to cry. She covered her face with her tender hands, hiding her tears. As he stood there helplessly watching the sad, elegant woman, a strange feeling came to his hand. He involuntarily moved his hand to his back pocket as if it were possessed. He carefully removed the bizarre paintbrush that was once again glowing with a mystical aura. As he stared at the glowing brush in his hand, his eyes suddenly lit up. He was struck with inspiration. While the elegant woman continued to weep, a gentle tap on her knee interrupted her. As she removed her hands from her flushed and tear-filled face, a bouquet of vibrantly colored flowers sat in the forefront of her vision. Her tears stopped when she saw the young boy holding the flowers, gesturing to hand them to her with a pleasant smile on his face.

"What is the meaning of this?" Lisa asked.

"Aren't flowers supposed to make girls smile?" the boy kindly asserted with a smile.

The elegant woman looked at the boy with a bewildered face. Her cheeks began to turn red, like two budding roses ready to blossom.

"W-why thank you," Lisa said. "You are too kind."

The elegant woman kindly accepted the bouquet of vibrantly colored flowers from the boy.

"I know Mr. da Vinci really made you feel special, but you don't need him to tell you that," the boy asserted. "Everyone is a work of art. Even the *Mona Lisa* was once a blank canvas, which means that we are all just masterpieces waiting to be painted … even you. So just keep smiling!"

The elegant woman was at a loss for words. Tears began reforming in the corners of her glossy eyes. A strange feeling overcame her as the boy's words resonated in her ears and in her spirit. No one had ever made her feel this way since her painter, Leonardo da Vinci. The corners of her lips softly shifted upward, bringing a modest smile to her rosy face.

"Thank you, child," Lisa said with a smile. "Your words have truly moved me and have given me a new reason to smile. What could I possibly do to show you my gratitude?"

The boy looked down to his lap as he removed the photograph

from the pocket of his hooded sweatshirt. He examined the photograph of the unfamiliar woman holding a newborn baby. Then he turned his attention to an oddly familiar boy standing next to the unfamiliar woman and her child. The boy in the picture seemed to be around the age of six, perhaps, and looked as if he could not be happier. As he continued to look at the photograph of strangers, tears filled his eyes. A worried expression came to the elegant woman's face as the boy began to sniffle and whimper.

"Dear child, what troubles you so?" Lisa asked.

The boy wiped the tears from his eyes with his sleeve and composed himself.

"I'm lost," the boy softly wept, "and I don't know what I'm supposed to do."

The elegant woman smiled at the sobbing boy. She rose from her chair and glided down to the boy like an angelic being descending from her heavenly throne. She gently embraced the boy in her motherly arms. The warmth of her radiant glow comforted the boy, putting him at ease.

"Be silent, child," Lisa softly said. "Your journey is nearing its end. The answer you seek is closer than you know."

The sniffling boy gently pulled away from the elegant woman and looked into her eyes.

"I don't understand," the boy said. "I've gone so many places and have come so far, but I still don't know who I am. I don't know what I should do."

The elegant woman smiled at the boy and placed one hand on his head and the other on his shoulder. She closed her eyes and giggled, delicately pulling him back into her arms. Her warm, radiant skin began to shine with a golden hue.

"Keep searching, child," Lisa softly said with a smile. "You must remember:

"It matters not how far you climb—
The answer will come in due time."

"I don't understand." The boy sniffled.

"You will, my child," Lisa said. "In due time."

As the elegant woman squeezed the boy closely to her heart, the glow of her warm, radiant skin intensified, enthralling the two in a golden aura. The blinding brightness continued to grow, absorbing the surrounding world in its comforting light. As the boy opened his eyes, he saw a painting of a rather elegant, smiling woman mounted on the wall before him. He carefully read the label underneath the painting to discover it to be the *Mona Lisa* by Leonardo da Vinci. His eyes widened in awe as he stood before the legendary painting for the very first time. It was not every day that one got the opportunity to stand before the *Mona Lisa*, after all. A whimsical smile came to his face as he gazed at the woman's enigmatic smile.

"She is truly a masterpiece."

Chapter 12

In the Stroke of Time

Anonymous

As memories fade from my head,
I begin to forget the past.
Toward the future I look ahead.
Finally, I am free at last;
The past no longer defines me.

* * * ??:?? * * *

Though the magnificent grace of the *Mona Lisa* had captured his imagination, the boy could feel his last memories slipping away. The art spirit's spell continued to spread through every crevice of his mind like the moss that crept through the cracks of the Arts District's walls, slowly eroding his memories. He could no longer remember anything about his past as the memories of his friends, family and loved ones faded into the darkness. Even his short-term memory was besieged by the corrosive spell, and he could no longer remember the details of his journey. The boy woefully hung his head and closed his eyes in defeat, ready to accept his fate. As he cleared his mind of all thought, he heard the taunting ticks and tocks of a clock echoing through the empty halls of his mind. He suddenly realized that he had no idea how long it had been since this horrid nightmare had begun. He had not seen a clock since the menacing clock tower of the Arts District struck the hour of midnight. The boy opened his eyes and began curiously searching the walls for the hidden clock emitting the tormenting ticks and tocks, yet there was no clock to be found. As he scanned the walls, his eyes stumbled across a rather bizarre painting of several clocks mounted on the wall. He gazed into the painting with a furrowed brow, attempting to interpret its meaning as the steady tempo of ticks and tocks began to amplify in volume. The boy continued to gaze at the painting, and the voice of a woman echoed in his head.

In due time.

The boy turned his attention to the label under the painting to discover its name. It was *The Persistence of Memory* by Salvador Dalí. The boy reflected on the rather peculiar name of the piece. He turned his attention back to the *Mona Lisa*. He examined the smiling woman closely, studying every part of her, looking for some sort of clue. His vision honed to her eyes as she stared directly forward with a fixed gaze. As the boy turned his head to match the line of sight of the smiling woman, he realized that she was staring directly at *The Persistence of Memory*. He reverted his attention back to the bizarre painting of several clocks. He had never seen it before, and yet he could not shake the feeling that it was calling out to him, hypnotizing him with its tantalizing ticks and tocks. With his eyes fixed on the painting, the boy carefully removed the paintbrush from his back pocket. He slowly raised the paintbrush to the painting with uncertainty. To his surprise, the paintbrush started glowing just as the sequence of ticks and tocks began flocculating and speeding out of control. With no other ideas, the boy emotionlessly entered into the painting, throwing caution to the wind with no inhibitions left.

Moments later, the boy arrived in a bizarre, barren desert. His throat almost dried immediately with only a single breath of the arid air. He could feel the heat of the scorched earth searing through the soles of his shoes, as if he were standing on molten rock. His eyes panned across the vast wasteland, and there seemed to be no presence of any other creatures. Off in the distance, he saw a wooden dresser. With no other human landmarks in sight, he made his way toward it. As he approached the dresser that lay in the middle of the desert, he heard a faint and mysterious sound.

What is that? the boy thought to himself.

As he got closer to the abandoned dresser, the strange sound began to grow louder. He then noticed a clock lying on its back that appeared to be suspended in midair. The boy's face wrinkled with confusion as he approached the levitating clock.

"It sounds like … snoring?" the boy whispered to himself.

Just as the boy thought he had identified the mysterious sound, he stumbled over a large object lying on the ground, causing him to fall. He propped himself up on his rear and scanned the ground around him to locate the object that caused his blunder, but there was nothing there. There was only the snorting and snuffling of snoring. The boy reached his hand out toward the sound and touched a large object that was invisible to the eye. Suddenly, a bizarre creature appeared before him. Its flat, distorted body lay draped across the sand like a magic carpet, gently waving in the hot desert wind. The figure and shape of the creature was vague, as its uncanny appearance seemed to be neither human nor beast but rather something in between. Its large, lone eye remained closed as several rake-like eyelashes protruded from its lid. The snorting and snuffling snoring seemed to be coming from what appeared to be its nose. The nostrils subtly expanded and retracted to the beat of its breathing. The startled boy sat there muted, afraid to awaken the creature from its slumber. Fortunately, the creature seemed to be in a dreamlike state, unaffected by the world around it. As the boy quietly stood, he discovered three more clocks in the area. One clock rested on the branch of a tree that peculiarly grew from the dresser, while another clock lay next to an antiquated pocket watch atop the dresser. As the boy got a closer look at the clocks, he noticed several ants picking at the pocket watch as if it were a discarded piece of fruit. Perplexed, the boy leaned in closer to examine the ant-covered pocket watch. His eyes widened in disbelief as the pocket watch began melting and dripping like hot wax from a burning candle. The boy swung his attention to the other clocks as they too began melting away. Alarmed, the boy began questioning the world around him, when suddenly he felt a light tap on his foot. He looked down to see a small splash of paint splattered on the tip of his shoe. The puzzled boy observed the paint splatter with peering eyes, noticing that it was the same color as his skin. His examination was shortly interrupted by the sensation of water gently dripping from his fingertips. As he raised his hand into his line of vision, a mortified expression came to his face.

"Wha … w-w-what's going on?" the boy hollered.

The boy gripped his forearm, attempting to calm the shaking of his melting right hand. Terror entered into his eyes as his forearm began melting through his left hand, as if it were made of mud. In a hysterical panic, the boy reached into his back pocket for the paintbrush, only for it to melt right through his fingers onto the ground. The boy fell to his knees, hopelessly washing away like some troublesome graffiti. The world around him began to liquefy. Tears of his very existence poured down into his wet, dripping hands, pointlessly, as if he were crying in the rain.

"So ... this is your limit?" a mysterious voice interjected.

The boy whipped his head up as the extravagantly dressed and ghastly man lingered before him. The art spirit appeared to be unaffected by the decaying world as he looked down upon the melting boy with displeasure. The boy looked upon the art spirit with desperate eyes as a mournful expression came to the spirit's face.

"True art is limitless," Palette somberly asserted. "Such frivolous things as time and space cannot confine its boundless beauty. It is only through art that one can exist in this world for eternity, for true art is timeless! Only true artists can rise above all others, for they are the chosen few who speak the Sacred Language of Art."

After hearing the art spirit's words, the boy looked to his hands. They were no longer melting away. In fact, his body appeared as if nothing had happened. As the boy stood, the remains of the world around them melted away, leaving them standing in a vastly void, white space. The boy looked in all directions, seeing nothing but empty whiteness. He turned his attention back to the art spirit as his monologue continued.

"It [Sacred Language] is a journey through the emotion, the passion, the present, and the creative experience that takes place in one's mind. Sacred Language is a place where silence is golden and knowledge depends through enlightenment! Art extrudes passion, which can only be felt if one has experienced inner spirituality. Sacred Language is a desire to be that changes with each individual's perception, speaking in everlasting words to the soul[7] ... however, such ideals have been lost."

The boy listened intently to the art spirit's words, leaving him speechless. The silent pause was shortly interrupted as the art spirit summoned the replica portrait once again. The boy's heart sank upon looking at the painting. He stood frozen, with all emotion stripped from his face as he gazed upon the virtually blank canvas. Only the faint scraps of what was once the image of a young boy remained, surrounded by nothing but blank, white canvas.

"It would seem that your time has run out, my dear child," Palette declared. "Have you found what you were looking for?"

A gloomy air overcame the boy. There were no words that came to his mouth. He shamefully lowered his head, clenching his fists in disappointment. The art spirit looked upon the boy with dissatisfaction.

"'Tis truly a shame," Palette solemnly asserted. "But alas, you can say farewell to the person you once were, forever. How very disappointing."

As the art spirit disgracefully shook his head, the last remains of the replica portrait faded away.

"All that remains is a blank canvas," Palette asserted. "What ever shall you do now?"

As the boy clenched his fists tighter and tighter, he firmly shut his eyes, desperately fighting back his tears.

"What shall you do?" Palette shouted.

The boy shuddered at the thunderous roar of the art spirit's voice. He stood there, motionless, unwilling to back down yet still without words to say. His weary eyelids could no longer withstand the pressure of the floodwaters, and the levees finally ruptured, drowning his face in tears. Finally accepting his defeat, the boy sorrowfully turned away from the art spirit and began walking toward his eternity of loneliness in the limbo world. He wiped his face with his sleeve but to no avail, as the relentless downpour of his sobbing tears could not be contained. The vast expanse of emptiness was a lot like the Arts District in many ways—desolate and abandoned. It was no place for someone with a bright future, to say the least. However, none of that mattered now, as the boy would never return to his former life in the Arts District. Never to remember Officer Bluebell, who looked out for him time after time, keeping him out of trouble. Never to remember the T3s, who took him in and treated him like one of their own. Never to remember Coal's loud voice, always hogging the spotlight. Never to remember Grayson's moans and groans about how everything was such a chore. Never to remember Ash, their fearless leader and the one who would one day tag the entire world black and white. Never to remember Pastel, who introduced him to the magnificent world of art. Though he had known Pastel for a short time, the boy had grown rather fond of him. He was so talented and so passionate about art and life, and he made the boy his apprentice when he could have just had him sent to juvenile jail. But he didn't. Instead, he took the boy in. He saw something special in the boy that the boy could not see himself. He made the boy feel special. As the boy continued to walk toward the nothingness, he suddenly came to a stop. The tears ceased flowing as his woeful weeping came to an end. The art spirit peered at him from a distance with curious eyes, closely reading the boy's actions.

"Could it be?" Palette whispered to himself.

As the boy came to a stop and ceased his crying, a thoughtful look came to his face, and one, lone memory returned to his mind. He wiped his face for the last time, replacing the pity in his eyes with determination. He slowly turned back to face the art spirit, who watched with eager eyes.

"Have you already forgotten, my dear child?" Palette asserted with a fiendish chuckle. "You are nothing more than a blank canvas!"

The boy gazed upon the blank canvas that once contained his memories of the past. A feeling of nostalgia came over his body, softening his eyes for just an instant before returning his sharp, unwavering gaze back to the art spirit. A slight, sinister grin came to the art spirit's face as the boy stood tall before him.

"All that remains is a blank canvas!" Palette roared.

The art spirit's voice ripped through the air, rocking and rattling the entire world, yet the boy stood unshaken. A subtle smile came to the boy's face as he closed his eyes and silently reflected on his one and only memory.

"You know, you're right," Huey proclaimed. "I may just be a blank canvas, but that just means that I'm a work in progress … a potential masterpiece! I just had to decide what to paint. That's half the battle, you know."

A wicked grin came to the art spirit's face as he stared into the boy's resolute eyes. The boy's fearless face was matched only by the sheer confidence of his stance, a manner in which the art spirit had never seen the boy stand. His back was rigid, his fists were clenched, his head held high. Even the boy's persistent stuttering was no more. Who was this boy that now stood before the spirit of art?

"My, my, my, you don't say!" Palette asserted with a wicked grin. "So then, child, what shall you do now?"

A hush filled the air as the boy paused for several seconds without responding. The art spirit eagerly watched the boy with expecting eyes, salivating in anticipation of his response. Finally, the boy took a few assertive steps forward. He slowly bent over and picked up the bizarre paintbrush off of the ground. He gently brushed its bristles, cleaning it of any dust that may have gotten on it. He carefully removed the photograph from the pocket of his hooded sweatshirt and held it in front of him. As the boy gazed at the photograph with inspired eyes, the paintbrush began to glow with a familiar, mystical aura. A sly grin came to the boy's face as he looked up to the art spirit, mirroring his wicked grin.

"Isn't it obvious?" Huey asserted. "I'm going to paint, of course!"

The art spirit broke out into a spirited cackle, thoroughly pleased at the boy's response.

"You are quite a piece of work, Huey, my boy!" Palette rejoiced.

Majestic flocks of vibrantly colored birds began bursting from the art spirit's feathery shawl and soaring overhead, painting the sky with a magnificent collage of colors and hues, like a floating botanical garden hanging in the sky. He then summoned a Japanese woodblock printing of a massive ocean wave entitled *The Great Wave off Kanagawa* (神奈川沖浪裏) by Hokusai.

Titanic tidal waves of water began surging out of the printing. Schools of miraculous fish, with their shining and shimmering scales, swam below the boy's feet, transforming the floor into a vast, oceanic sanctuary, decorated with vividly colored coral reefs and aquatic creatures. The boy looked in awe as the art spirit began to shift and morph into a long serpentine form that slithered through the air like a snake. The refracting light on the creature's shimmering, scaly feathers sent waves of rainbows down the length of its reptilian body. Its elongated snout bore its perfectly sculpted, white marble fangs as psychedelic flames from its fiery breath seeped through the crevices of its wicked grin. Its large, flaring nostrils released clouds of colorful mist, coating its surroundings in a thin layer of spray paint with each snorting exhale. Its flowery, oriental mane fully bloomed with sweet-scented cherry blossoms, filling the breeze with its peaceful, pink petal rain as the bristly tip of its tail writhed and wriggled, dripping with vibrant colors like a paint-daubed brush. It glared at the boy with its gleaming, green eyes that glowed like two jade, cat's eye marbles. The boy stood there with an open-mouthed smile and outstretched arms, exhilarated as the feathered serpent creature flapped its mighty wings, whipping his body with great gusts of wind. The boy remained awestricken as the world around him was transformed into a breathtaking paradise like a mural in motion. This was the boundless beauty of which Palette, the spirit of art, spoke of, for such a remarkable sight was truly timeless and limitless indeed.

"Go forth, my child!" Palette triumphantly roared. "Your masterpiece awaits the hand of a true artist!"

The boy's face lit up with delight as he dashed toward the blank canvas with his glowing paintbrush in hand, ready to paint his everlasting story. Glowing sashes of paint formed around him, tailing him like neon streaks of light. A sash of paint miraculously transformed into an aerosol spray can as the boy grabbed it in his open hand. The boy filled the air with the pitter-pattering of his footsteps and the clanking and crackling of his aerosol spray can as he made a final leap into the world of his own blank canvas, with a fresh start and a clean slate. He had finally found the place where the shackles of the past could no longer confine him—the perfect place for someone with a troubled past and a bright future.

Chapter 13
Back to the Drawing Board

If you hear a voice within you say
"you cannot paint," then by all means
paint, and that voice will be silenced.
-VINCENT VAN GOGH

"**M**agnifique!" Pastel cheered. "The care within each delicate stroke! The attention to detail! The love! The passion! Truly magnificent!"

The tall, slender man basked in awe as he and the boy stood before an extraordinary painting that the boy had worked through the night to complete.

"How did you do all of this in only one night?" Pastel asked.

"I guess time flies when you're having fun," Huey replied. "It's like you said; it's easy to get lost in the art."

Pastel smiled, patting the boy on the shoulder. "You must tell me. What was the inspiration behind this magnificent work of art?"

The boy looked at the tall, slender man for a moment and smiled, reaching into the pocket of his hooded sweatshirt. He carefully pulled out a photograph of a woman, a newborn baby, and a six-year-old boy in a hospital room and handed it to Pastel. The photograph was identical to the boy's painting.

"And what do we have here?" Pastel asked.

"It's a picture of my family," Huey said.

Pastel looked up from the photograph, lowering his dark, circular sunglasses and staring at the boy. As he began to remember the disagreement he and the boy had the day before, he suddenly understood why the boy responded in such a hostile manner.

"I'm sorry, Huey," Pastel said. "I did not mean to pry."

"It's okay," Huey said with a smile. "All this time, I've been so afraid of letting go of the past that I lost my way. I'll always cherish the memories of my past, but I will no longer allow them to define me. It's time for me to move on."

A shocked expression came to Pastel's face. He was stunned by the maturity of the boy's words.

"I would like to tell you about them," Huey said with a smile.

"And I would love to hear about them," Pastel responded.

Pastel hunched over next to the boy, and they each held an edge of the photograph. The boy pointed to the six-year-old boy in the picture.

"This is me," Huey said. "I was only six back when this was taken."

"Wow!" Pastel exclaimed. "And look at you now. You have really grown up to become quite a fine young man!"

The tall, slender man playfully ruffled the boy's hair, and the two started laughing. After their laughter died down, the boy pointed to the woman in the picture.

"And this is my mom," Huey said. "She passed away shortly after this picture was taken. The doctors said she had complications recovering after giving birth. This is the last memory of her that I have."

The room became still as neither the boy nor Pastel spoke. Emotions ran through the air, though they were neither somber nor sorrowful. There was only a feeling of peace and serenity as the two partook in the moment of silence.

"She was rather beautiful," Pastel said. "A true work of art!"

The boy looked up to Pastel and softly smiled at his compliment.

"Thank you," Huey replied. "She was as pretty as the *Mona Lisa*."

The boy and Pastel exchanged smiles, both in agreement with the boy's remark. Turning his attention back to the photograph, Pastel fixed his eyes to the small, newborn baby that rested gently nestled in the arms of the boy's mother.

"And who might this young fellow be?" Pastel asked.

A gloomy look came to the boy's face.

"That's my little brother ..." Huey somberly said. "After my mother died from giving birth to him, we were separated. He was smaller than normal and had to stay under the hospital's care for a long time. Since I was older, I was placed in foster care and ended up being forced to move from place to place. I haven't seen my little brother since he was born, but I know he's out there somewhere. He just turned six this past April. His name is Dorian, and I'm going to find him someday. If only I could get out of the Arts District ..."

Pastel looked upon the boy with astonishment as the boy diverted his gaze to the floor. He could not help but wonder how much pain and loneliness the boy must have gone through his entire life. He stood there at a loss for words. He began scanning the large, open studio room, placing his gaze on the several sketchbooks and paint-daubed canvases scattered across the tabletops and the floor. He gently closed his eyes and took in a deep breath of air. As he continued to ponder, a serene, blissful smile came to his face. He opened his eyes and turned his attention back to the boy, placing one hand on his head and the other on his shoulder. The boy slowly looked up at Pastel.

"Huey," Pastel said, "why don't you come with me?"

The boy looked at him with a puzzled expression.

"As a traveling artist, I have galleries and studios all across the country," Pastel explained. "For my next art tour, why don't you tag along? I can show you a world outside of the Arts District's walls. A world filled with magnificent art! And if Dorian is out there somewhere, then we shall find him. Together."

The boy's eyes and mouth widened, wider than they had ever before. He looked at the tall, slender man in disbelief, unable to process what he just heard.

"We will have to run it by Officer Bluebell, of course," Pastel asserted with a sincere smile. "We will call it a field trip … vital for your creative growth. You are my apprentice, after all!"

The boy's eyes began to tear, and his wide, gaping mouth turned into a face-consuming smile. Not a single word escaped the boy's lips as he vigorously hugged Pastel, breaking out into tears of joy. Pastel embraced the weeping boy in his arms with a genuine smile. A match made in heaven.

* * * 5:00 p.m. Friday * * *

The boy waved to Pastel from down the street as he made his way back home after a long, adventure-filled day at Spirit Rise. Pastel joyfully waved back as the boy made his departure, and as he turned to lock the front door, a voice called out to him from the distance.

"I almost forgot!" Huey shouted from afar. "I 'refined' my master-piece on the side of your building! I think you'll appreciate it!"

A baffled expression came to Pastel's face as the boy ran off. He walked down the block of Spirit Rise toward the vandalized wall, wondering what the boy could have possibly meant. As he rounded the corner of the building, he abruptly came to a stop. He lowered his dark, circular sunglasses as his wide-eyed gaze marveled at the breathtaking graffiti mural tagged on the wall.

"You truly are a piece of work, Huey," Pastel whispered.

As Pastel looked upon the vandalized wall, he began to chuckle. He shadily tilted his suave, fedora-styled hat over his eyes as a wicked grin came to his face. From his raised hand, a vibrantly colored feather gently drifted to the ground from the sleeve of his paisley-patterned shirt of many colors.

"You are no longer lost, my dear child," Pastel said with a wicked grin. "I am glad that you have found what you were looking for!"

Notes

1   Arthur Lubow, "Edvard Munch: Beyond The Scream," *Smithsonian Magazine*, March 2006.

2   John Lichfield, "The Moving of the Mona Lisa," *The Independent*, April 2, 2005.

3   Juliet; William Shakespeare's *Romeo and Juliet.*

4   *David* (Michelangelo, 1501–1504); masterpiece Renaissance sculpture.

5   *The Sistine Chapel ceiling* (Michelangelo, 1508–1512), a cornerstone work of High Renaissance art.

6   Information on the *Mona Lisa,* the woman: http://www.nbcnews.com/science/science-news/mona-lisa-researchers-work-find-woman-behind-famous-painting-n93491

7   Excerpts from Anthony Liggins's Artist's Statement.

Other Works by Ryan Adkins

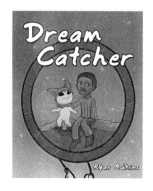

It is the first day of school for six-year-old Dorian Hubble, and making new friends is so much trouble! While Dorian uses his imagination to dream of rockets, Martians, and outer space stations, his classmates laugh, giggle, and grin. Dorian feels sad and wonders if he will ever fit in.

Later that night, Dorian uses his dream catcher to wish for a friend, with the hope that his loneliness will disappear. But when his wish comes true, Dorian learns that if he believes in himself, even his wildest dreams can come true. As he takes a journey through the beautiful world of dreams, Dorian finds strength and happiness in a magical land filled with creatures both big and small!

Dream Catcher is a captivating children's story that encourages children to dare to be different, chase their dreams, and discover the power of their imaginations!

CPSIA information can be obtained at www.ICGtesting.com
Printed in the USA
LVOW12s1513300615

444433LV00002BA/7/P